AnaisImprint
Miami, Florida

This one's for my girlfriends.

Fifty Ways to Leave Your Husband

a novel

by

k.c. wilder

Meredith —

Keep being BOLD!

"K.c. wilder"

AnaisImprint
Miami, Florida

Chapter **One**

"So, I think that's it," I said to Skip. "Car's packed and ready to go."

I stood in the kitchen, looking out through the open sliding doors at my husband. He was stretched out on a lounge chair midway between the house and the pool, sunglasses slightly askew, a single flip-flop dangling from his big toe. I wondered for a second if he'd fallen asleep. Then he sat up and ran a hand through his hair - it was thinning, but what was left of it was still blonde and curly and tended to make him look younger than his forty-six years.

He was handsome, always had been and always would be. I caught myself putting a hand to my hair, shifting my posture, smoothing my skirt. It was an awkward habit I'd had ever since meeting Skip eighteen years earlier. As if I could just run a hand over my hair, my clothes, and somehow measure up.

"Sorry," Skip said, standing and crossing the patio. "I was gonna load the car for you." He gave me a peck on the cheek and a light swat on the rear end as he walked past me into the kitchen. It wasn't a sign of affection between us. These were his go-to moves with far too many women. Living with Skip was like living in an episode of *Mad Men*. "You got everything in there okay? Tennis gear and fifty pairs of shoes and whatever?"

He chuckled to himself, and I refrained from comment. I did not play tennis. And I had only packed six pairs of shoes.

I watched as he poured himself a Bloody Mary from the pitcher on the countertop. He wore khaki shorts and he'd thrown on yesterday's Brooks Brothers shirt, rumpled from a night on the floor. I had no idea when he'd gotten in last night, or where he'd been, for that matter.

In other words, it was a typical Saturday morning at the Wolcott residence.

"I texted the boys," I told him. "Max has lacrosse practice. Sounds like he's settling in. Eli hasn't responded yet, but I think he might've had sailing this morning."

"Jesus," Skip sighed, taking a long slurp of his drink. "Quit hovering already. They're at one of the best boarding schools in New England. Do you hear yourself? Lacrosse, sailing. It's not exactly prison, you know. My brothers and I all survived."

And look how well you all turned out.

I bit my tongue before the thought could slip out. The

Wolcott men were successful by certain measures. They were handsome and had plenty of money and fancy homes and cars and boats. But they were also all alcoholics and philanderers and, frankly, not very nice people. Skip was the only one not to have been divorced, and given the overall trajectory of our marriage, I wasn't sure he'd be able to maintain that distinction. To say things had been rocky between us would have been an understatement.

It was likely the reason I was more antsy than usual to begin my vacation with Tamara. Our annual girls' escape. I *needed* escape. Lately I couldn't seem to feel comfortable in my own skin. I needed to talk to Tam about just what the hell I was going to do now that both boys were out of the house. I didn't think Skip and I would do well being alone together.

"Go on," he said, shooing me toward the door. "Go meet your crazy friend and have a good time spending my money. Get a makeover at the spa or something. Botox, or whatever it is you girls do when you hit forty. The boys will be fine." He paused as we reached the front door, then winked at me. "Just don't do anything I wouldn't do."

I cringed. Sometimes Skip's sense of humor hit too close to home. I never ceased to worry about what he might be doing when I wasn't with him. Which was a bit of an issue, since we'd arguably spent most of our marriage apart. His office was in Boston, so that was where he stayed during the week. And even when he was home, he was always making plans to head out somewhere else.

"There's chicken in the fridge," I said uselessly. "And

salad. Don't forget the salad."

I knew I would come home in a week to uneaten chicken and wilted, mushy salad. But at least I'd tried.

"I'll probably just eat in Newport," he said.

He meant with his mother, Kitty, my least-favorite person on this planet. Tamara joked that Kitty could be the solution to global climate change. "One glance from that woman and the polar ice caps would freeze over again," she'd said. She may have been right.

Skip gave me another quick peck on the cheek and swat on the rear, and I watched him disappear into the house, a gust of wind slamming the door shut behind him. I stood there for a moment, rattled by a swirl of feelings I couldn't quite name.

I had the top down on the car, ready to go. I dropped my handbag onto the passenger seat and slid behind the wheel. This was my favorite time of year. September. Most of the tourists had left the Rhode Island shoreline, but the sunshine and warmth remained. I was looking forward to the drive from Jamestown to Watch Hill. I tucked a hat gently over my hair, determined not to arrive at Ocean Manor looking like Bridget Jones. I put the car into gear and started down my long driveway, thinking suddenly and vividly of the trip we'd made just three days earlier, when we delivered the boys to Morefield Academy.

Eli had ridden in the convertible with me, and of course, Max had ridden with Skip. We each had our mini-me, Skip and I, though I sometimes wished we could trade places, just for a day. I wondered what it was like to be the fun parent paired with the fun child.

Eli was so practical, so orderly and solemn. He was quiet and studious and obedient. Even as a toddler, he'd been that way. While other mothers were scrambling to baby-proof their homes and trading tales of the "terrible twos," I would simply explain to Eli why he couldn't do something, he'd say, "Oh," and that would be the end of it.

At fourteen, he was beginning his second year at Morefield, and he'd told me on the drive that he wasn't happy there. When I suggested alternatives, he shrugged. "Yeah, right," he'd said sarcastically. "Run that one by Dad." I couldn't think of a thing to say, so we made the rest of the trip in silence, trailing along behind Skip's Range Rover. Eli wore earbuds and played music on his iPhone that was so loud and angry I could hear it from the driver's seat. I'd wondered for the millionth time if this was normal teen angst or if I should be concerned.

Max, in contrast, was lively and outgoing. He'd inherited Skip's patrician good looks and his impulsive, energetic nature. From just about birth, he'd been impossible to keep still. He'd never tolerated hugs or any sort of mothering, which somehow made me crave it more. When he was little, I'd try to gather him in my arms or kiss him on the top of the head. He'd wriggle away, all determination and defiance. He played every sport imaginable, excelling at each and finally settling on hockey and lacrosse as his favorites. At twelve going on thirteen, this was his first year at Morefield. When we left him at his dormitory, he'd already made friends and was talking with them about learning to play rugby. He was so much like Skip it hurt.

I shook myself out of my reverie as I reached the gates and clicked them open. In the rear view mirror, the hulk of weathered New England architecture that had been my home since the boys were babies loomed large. It was a turn-of-the-century summer home with wide porches and slanted, creaking floorboards, multiple staircases and endless cupboards and nooks and crannies. Some of my favorite memories were of rainy days when the boys were little, the draperies hanging heavy in the humid air, the smells of salt and earth drifting in through the open windows. We'd play hide-and-seek, their little feet scampering overhead while I sat on a stair with my face in my hands, counting. We'd bake cookies and play board games, and I felt a sense of comfort and happiness that had since eluded me. The house seemed empty as I drove away from it in the bright late-summer morning. The lawn rolled gracefully to the rocky water's edge, and sunlight glinted off the small whitecaps raised by the gathering winds.

As I pulled out onto the road, the breeze sent a whiff of delicious fragrance from the rare witch hazel shrubs along our driveway. They were a gift from our neighbor Wally, a semi-retired attorney and gardening enthusiast. Just in case he was outside, I honked the horn and waved as I drove past. He was seventy-nine years old and a bit of a curmudgeon, but Wally was my best friend on the island.

The irony of leaving my seaside home for another waterfront location just forty minutes away was not lost on me. But this was the fourth year Tamara and I were making our little escape to Ocean Manor. We'd chosen it initially because of its proximity to both my home in Jamestown and hers in Stonington, Connecticut. At the time, Tamara had been pregnant with her third baby. She'd been nervous leaving her two little guys home with Howard, and while I had a nanny to keep tabs on Max and Eli, who was going to keep tabs on Skip? So we'd fallen into our little getaway close to home, and each year we'd extended our stay. This year we'd booked a whole week, primarily because Tamara knew I'd be a basket case with both boys off at school. She'd promised to keep me "mightily distracted with booze and pool boys." After all, what are friends for?

    I cranked up the stereo as I crossed the bridge.

    "Stop worrying," I admonished myself aloud, mostly because I wasn't sure what, exactly, I was worrying about.

    I had thought last year would be the tough one, with Eli off at boarding school for the very first time, but I still had Max to keep me busy. His never-ending schedule of sporting and social events made me feel like a taxi driver. We'd even kept Lola, the nanny, employed in her live-in position, though it seemed somewhat comical to me. My full-time job was being a mother. How much help did I need, really, with only one child still at home?

    As I approached Westerly, I turned off Route One and made my way into Watch Hill. I was singing along with Blondie when the song cut out and my iPhone rang through my speakers. I glanced at Tamara's name on the screen, smiled, and punched the Bluetooth button.

"Hey you!" I said enthusiastically.

"Hey," Tamara said, her voice a notable shade darker. Her lingering Boston accent infused the single syllable with attitude, as always, but even so I got the sense that something was wrong. "Where the fuck are you? It sounds like a fucking wind tunnel."

Fuck was Tamara's favorite word.

"Sorry," I apologized, checking my mirrors and flipping on my directional. "I'm in the summer car, and I've got the top down."

I pulled over, as far onto the narrow shoulder as possible.

"The summer car," Tamara snorted, teasing. "That still cracks me the fuck up. Only you would have a Bimmer for every season."

I laughed. She and her husband Howard got a new car at least once a year, only they were cool hipster VWs or Priuses or Smart Cars. Same thing, really. Different approach.

"Is that better?" I asked as the wind noise subsided.

"Much better. But listen. I have bad news for our girls' getaway. Really bad news."

"No," I groaned. I was not in a bad-news frame of mind. "Tell me you're just stuck in traffic."

"I wish," Tamara sighed. "Nope. Nana went and kicked the bucket about two hours ago."

I was stunned.

Nana was Tamara's ancient, sweet, Alzheimer's-addled grandma. I had at least a thousand good memories of her from the time I was college-age until now. Tamara's property in Stonington had originally belonged to Nana. The guest cottage had become Nana's place over the years. I knew her health had declined, but I hadn't realized how seriously. I had somehow taken for granted that she'd always be there.

"Oh no, Tam," I said, blinking at the tears in my eyes. "I'm so sorry."

"Yeah, well," she grumbled, exhaling, "She was ninety-eight years old. Not exactly a surprise, right? But to be honest, I'm a little ticked with her at the moment. Ninety-eight fucking years old, and she couldn't hang on for just one more week? I mean, this little getaway is our tradition, you and me, and I seriously need to get *away*. The kids are driving me fucking batty."

"Oh, Tam," I said, laughing through my tears. "It's not like Nana died on purpose. I'm sure she would have wanted you to have your getaway as much as anyone. I mean, I love your boys, you know I do, but they're a handful, and no one knows that, ah, *knew* that better than Nana."

Tamara's boys ranged in age from two and a half to eight. Tam and Howard subscribed to a theory of parenting that viewed any discipline as soul-crushing, and as a result, their kids were wilder than most feral animals.

"A handful!" Tamara chuckled. "You are too fucking nice. Do you know what the little fuckers did this morning while I was trying to pack?"

"I can't imagine," I said truthfully.

"Marcus and Warhol convinced Reed that the first step

in potty-training is shitting in the yard like the dog. So he did. And then – well, you know how Reed is about picking up – he went and got the pooper-scooper and carted the whole fucking mess into the house, proud as can be, to show me. Wynn ran out of the playroom and -bam! - straight into him. Shit everywhere. And there I am, halfway through cleaning it up, and Marcus starts yelling that Nana won't wake up. End result? I've got the guys from the funeral home tracking kid-shit through the house, going, 'Oh, ma'am, I'm so sorry – I think I stepped in something your dog did,' and I just fucking lose it. I mean, I laugh my head off like a crazy lady until I can finally catch my breath enough to tell the poor guy, 'No worries about the dog doo.' Honestly, I can't make this shit up."

I laughed in spite of myself. I could picture the scene all too clearly.

"Oh, Tam, I really am sorry," I said at last. "What can I do? Do you need a hand with the arrangements? Or with the boys?"

Please, dear god, let her not need my help with the boys.

I heard Tamara inhale and exhale again, slowly.

"Tam, are you smoking?"

"Yes."

"Pot? You're smoking pot?"

"Fuck, yes. What the hell kind of question is that? Did you not hear anything I just said? If smoking's not called for now, it never fucking is." She paused. "But hey, no, listen, I'm good here. Really. I mean, I guess that's the good thing about going at ninety-eight. Nana had all her arrangements in order.

But I'll still be stuck here. Mom's out of her tree. Keeps saying stupid shit about how God takes the good too young and so on. I mean, *hello*? *Ninety-eight fucking years old...* Anyway - you get the idea. Funeral's a week from Tuesday, though, to give Nate and Ian time to get out here. Why don't you just keep driving and enjoy some time on your own? I'll sneak out and meet you for drinks at some point, and then I'll see you at the service."

I started to protest, but Tamara interrupted.

"Look, I feel badly enough about fucking up our plans. I've already called the spa and booked you in for the full afternoon. They'll knead and prod and mud and wax every fucking inch of you, and they've got my AmEx to cover the damage. So go. I know you need the time away from Skip, and with the boys at school, what's stopping you?"

She was right. What was I going to do? Go home to the uncomfortable silences that had become the norm between me and Skip? Put my face into Max's pillow and weep over my baby, gone to boarding school? Cry over the way Eli, even as a baby, always seemed as though he was about fifty years old and didn't need a mom?

"Are you sure?" I asked at last.

"If I were any more sure, I'd be Heidi Macomber," Tamara said solemnly.

I laughed out loud. Heidi Macomber was our RA in our Mount Holyoke days. She was always right. Just ask her. She'd tell you.

"Call me tonight, okay? Whenever you get a minute."

"Sure thing," she said. "Just be tolerant. I'm half in the

bag now. No promises as to my condition later."

"Understandable," I said honestly.

We disconnected and I sat there for a few moments, cars whirring by and the sun warm on my shoulders. I thought of the house in Jamestown, so close I could easily turn the car around and just make my way back. What might Skip be doing by now? Napping by the pool? Maybe planning to meet his brother Steve on the boat in Newport later? Surely he was as grateful to have me gone as I was grateful to be out on my own. Such was the sad thing that our marriage had become.

I glanced at the floor in front of the passenger seat, where two novels lay, tossed almost as an afterthought. When Tam and I were together, there was little time for anything other than talk and silliness, but any weekend away by the sea seemed to beg for reading material, and so there they were. Now I could read them both, in solitude on a chaise at the beach.

I thought again of Max and Eli, and of the hollowness that was growing inside me. Ever since complications during my pregnancy with Eli forced me to quit my very first job after law school, all I had been was a mother. Well, a wife, too, I suppose, but it was being a mother that I considered my occupation. I'd worked at it, and when sometimes it seemed to require more work than I'd expected, or when it wasn't quite going well and I was tempted to count my failures, I'd remind myself of how short a time childhood is. A short time that, as it happened, was further shortened for me and my boys because of Skip and his family's damned obsession with boarding school. No, worse - because I lacked the backbone to fight the whole notion.

I thought of Max and Eli, of their faces as I said goodbye and left them - Max so happily dismissive and Eli stoic and brooding - and something in me crumbled. I couldn't decide if it was because I felt I'd abandoned them, or because I knew they were fine without me. I'd made their upbringing my career, and now I was adrift.

I realized it was myself I was feeling sorry for, not them. Thinking slightly less of myself, I put the car back into gear and continued my journey to Watch Hill. I aimed for Ocean Manor, and I didn't look back.

Ocean Manor had been the premier holiday destination in Watch Hill since 1868, and it was one of my favorite places on earth. Every time I turned into the drive at the main inn, I felt a mix of nostalgia, homecoming, and something more elusive and bittersweet that I couldn't fully put my finger on. I tended to think it was, at least in part, the relative proximity to my early childhood summer vacations (spent in a Misquamicut beach rental my parents prized for their one week of annual respite from work), coupled with the sort of luxury I'd become accustomed to since marrying into Skip's old New England family. The salt air, the casual elegance, the feeling of days gone by; all this I loved. The hotel had fallen into disrepair a decade earlier, requiring a complete rebuild, yet the historic feel of the property had been preserved to an extent that made our modern automobiles and attire and mannerisms seem an anachronism. I pulled up in front of the stately building and let well-mannered young men swoop in to take my car and my bags.

"Miss?" the valet called after me. "Your lipstick?"

I took a few steps back and squinted at the sparkly bubblegum-pink tube. It was the kind of cheap stuff a teenager might buy at CVS for $1.99. I shook my head.

"That's not mine," I said, slightly offended that he thought it was. But then, what did a twenty-something guy know about lipstick quality?

"It was in the car," he said. "I stepped on it by mistake. Sorry."

"It was in the car..." I repeated. I held out my hand and he placed the tube into my palm. It was cracked; evidence of his misstep. "Thank you," I said dully, the gears turning.

Skip had taken this car yesterday. He was playing golf with a client, he'd said. And then he'd come home god-knows-when. With a cheap pink lipstick rolling on the floor of the car. It was so cliche I almost dismissed it, but given Skip's track record, I'd have been a fool not to be suspicious. *Tap, tap, tap.* Another nail in the coffin of our marriage. I dropped the lipstick into my pocket and went to the front desk.

Tamara and I always stayed in a suite; the same one, if it was available when we booked: 313. I accepted the key and made my way upstairs, waiting for my bags to follow. I felt the pink lipstick there in my pocket as I walked, chafing against my thigh. How great would it have been to have Tamara here right now, Tamara who had never, ever warmed up to Skip and had a knack for making ballsy, inappropriate jokes of the most painful situations? I slipped the key in the lock and missed her a little bit more. I found our now-customary wine and cheese plate awaiting us, but it just didn't look appealing to me without Tam. I popped it into the mini-fridge. Then I went out onto the balcony and sat on one of the chairs. I looked out at the ocean and let out a long sigh. Was *I* cliche? Pathetic, even? I paused, wondering what Skip might be doing just then, and then I let the thought go. Did I really want to know?

A knock at the door drew me away from my thoughts.

"Your luggage, miss," a young man said carefully, his attractive, alarmingly youthful silhouette framed by the doorway.

I waved him inside, not missing the glance he gave me as he passed. Was he trying to be seductive? Was this what seduction looked like on someone so young and pretty, and when had I become too damn old to know?

Tamara had always told me that a woman could have any and every need met by the young men who spent their summers working here, and I always dismissed her with a laugh and a word or two. Now, though, I wondered.

"I'm Caleb," the young man said, reappearing without my luggage but wearing the most sly smile I've ever seen. "Is there anything else I can do for you, Mrs. Wolcott?"

It was obscene. Something in his tone and his expression told me that maybe Tamara was right, maybe this very young man was offering something more than just turn-down service and a mint on my pillow. It unsettled me. This boy was, by far, closer in age to Eli and Max than to me. What was he thinking? And were there really women - grown women, right here at this refined resort - who would take him up on his surreptitious offer?

"No, thank you very much, Caleb, I am just fine," I said stiffly.

"That you are," Caleb said, his voice just a whisper, a smirk at the corner of his lips. "Please - ask for me if there is anything at all I can do to make your stay more..." he paused "...comfortable."

I fumbled for a tip, which I slipped into his soft palm. He looked pointedly at my legs as he left. The boy gigolo. I let out a laugh before I could stop myself.

I have never been one of those pretty women who pretends not to know they're pretty. I know I'm no super model, but I also know I can turn heads. I know this mostly because I've improved with age. I was a gawky kid, a classic ugly duckling. I have red hair and freckles, and until about junior year of high school, I was always a foot taller than everyone else in my grade. I might as well have gone through school with a "kick me" sign pinned to my back. There's nothing like red hair, freckles and extreme height to delight and amuse bullies. For at least twelve years, I was a year-round Christmas gift for every insecure and mean-spirited asshole or Queen Bee in my public school system.

But trust me, ugly ducklings always know when they've turned into swans. At some point in college, I realized guys were checking me out. By the time I reached law school, Tamara had dubbed me "The Red Fox," and I was having a blast making up for lost time. That was when I met Skip, who I think homed in on me specifically because of all my suitors. Skip is the kind of man who always wants what other men want.

Until he has it, that is.

I returned to my chair on the balcony and watched as a woman at least a decade older than me trotted on high-heeled sandals to catch up to Caleb as he walked along a path below. She took hold of his arm, lightly, at the elbow. He said something and she let out an exaggerated laugh, tossing her head back and leaning into him. His hand touched her hip for a moment.

Oh Caleb, I know college is expensive, but really?

Again I felt the lipstick there in my pocket, the tacky thing irritating like a grain of sand you can't get out of your shoe.

I wandered back into the cottage and pulled the bottle of pinot grigio from the fridge. I glanced at my watch: 11:35 a.m. Not exactly cocktail hour, but what the hell? I opened the bottle and poured a glass. I was halfway back to the deck chair when the shrill ring of a phone startled me. Not my iPhone, which I'd set to sound like soft wind chimes when it rang. I swallowed my sip of wine and went to answer the in-room phone.

"Hello?"

"Mrs. Wolcott, this is Carrie at the front desk. Just checking in to be sure everything is satisfactory?"

"Yes, lovely."

My fingers fumbled absently with the pink lipstick in

my pocket.

Except that my husband is apparently once again sticking his dick into other women. Other than that, Carrie, everything is lovely.

"Very good. Please let us know if there is anything you need. And as a gentle reminder, your spa visit begins in forty-five minutes."

Right. Good thing Carrie-from-the-front-desk had called. I'd already forgotten.

"Of course. Thank you."

I hung up and fiddled with the phone, turning the volume of the ringer down. I checked my iPhone and found a text from Eli, typically abrupt: *Sailing. Max at LAX. Talk later.* It seemed Skip had been right; I'd been worrying for nothing. I headed back out to the deck chair, kicked off my shoes, and resumed sipping my wine.

I usually reserved drinking for certain types of occasions, and I had my own personal classification for each. For example, there was drinking with Tamara, which was Fun/Silly Drinking. That was the kind of drinking that, from college right up until now, could result in all-night discussions about crazy things, such as deciding which heads of state were do-able, or which hot celebrity women would most likely look like The Crypt Keeper in their senior years. Then there was Business Dinner Drinking. That meant nursing a single drink for an entire evening while trying to appear interested in whatever so-and-so's wife was saying, then driving home with Skip passed out in the passenger seat. And of course, there was Family-Gathering Drinking. That involved walking the fine line between drinking enough to tolerate the rowdy behavior of Skip and his brothers when gathered en masse, while remaining sharp enough to deflect Kitty's verbal barbs. It was a delicate balance.

I wasn't a fan of drinking alone, however, so I wasn't quite sure what I was doing when I finished one glass of wine and poured another. Pre-spa drinking? Was that a good idea? I was sure I was supposed to hydrate, but probably not with pinot grigio. I looked at the time and, caution be damned, downed the rest of the glass.

I arrived at the spa pretty solidly buzzed. For reasons I cannot explain, this made me proud of myself. It was like a private joke: *haha, I'm buzzed at the spa.* That was it. The joke in full. Funny only to me, as most jokes are when buzzed.

The massage was heavenly, though I think I may have moaned inappropriately at a few moments.

The mani/pedi went well: classic coral. Because even buzzed, I understood that it was late summer in Watch Hill.

Then came the bikini wax. My buzz lasted just long enough for me to make a poor decision, but not long enough to numb the pain that resulted.

That's right: I went with the Brazilian.

I have no idea why. Seriously. It wasn't until I had some strange woman applying hot wax to parts of me that hadn't seen the light of day since Eli was born (while I screamed, "Close the drapes!" in our room at Women & Infants; as if someone could have walked past our third floor window and looked in) that it occurred to me I'd made a very, very bad choice. A few tears and some undignified behavior later, I left the spa with what I imagined were the puffiest, most exposed girl-parts on the planet.

I sent a quick text to Tamara, telling her that I'd thoroughly enjoyed *most* of my spa visit.

Then I settled onto one of the queen-size beds in our suite, looking over at the empty bed that should have been Tamara's, and allowed feeling sorry for myself to replace feeling violated by the spa woman with the hot wax.

Chapter **Two**

I went bravely to the hotel restaurant at seven p.m. I
say, "bravely," because dining alone has never been my strong
suit. I'd dressed carefully, the intent being to look sophisticated
enough not to be pitied, but unremarkable enough to be
overlooked. I wanted to dine inconspicuously, just me and the
latest Chris Bohjalian novel. While I stood waiting near the
hostess' podium, scanning the dining room for a potentially safe
place to sit, I saw him.

He was good-looking, but in an understated way. There
were better-looking men right there, frankly, at the bar and in
the restaurant, but there was something about his demeanor. He
practically screamed nonchalance. (How's that for irony?) He

was wearing jeans and a linen button-down shirt, sleeves rolled to the elbow, in a place where all the other men were wearing sport coats and khakis and ties, because that was the dress code. But no one gave him any trouble, perhaps because he seemed to know everyone in the inn's employ. He chatted with the bartender as he sipped his drink, laughing and joking easily with everyone in the vicinity. The guy was clearly Someone, at least locally, but who?

I watched him, trying to peg the familiarity about him. I decided he looked a bit like a young Bryan Ferry, with his dark hair and debonair manner. But he was in much better shape than Bryan Ferry had ever been. Yes, this guy was as suave as Roxy Music's frontman in his glory days, but as fit as David Beckham. His posture alone gave away the rock-hard abs and tight ass beneath those well-worn blue jeans. I realized I was thinking of him as I hadn't thought of a man in ages: as one seriously hot dish I wouldn't mind sinking my teeth into.

Good god, what the hell was the matter with me? I thought back to the cheap pink lipstick still tucked into my pocket back at the suite. The source of the trouble. This was ridiculous.

I ducked back outside and took my phone from my purse. I called my home number and waited for Skip to answer. I'd just ask him. Maybe the client he'd been out playing golf with was female, and he'd just forgotten to mention that. Maybe I was getting all bent out of shape for nothing.

"Hello?" a female voice, familiar, sounded on the other end of the line.

As if from a distance, I heard Skip say something in the background. Then the sound became muffled, as if a hand had been clamped over the phone.

"Sorry!" The phone-answerer said to him in protest, barely audible. "Habit."

The fog that clouded my mind when I heard the voice but couldn't immediately place it cleared.

Lola, the boys' nanny for the past four years.

Lola, who'd moved out three weeks ago, when the boys were getting ready to head to Morefield and she was leaving for grad school at Boston University.

"Lola?" I choked into the phone.

"Eve?" Skip replied.

"What's Lola doing there?"

"She, ah, forgot some things and came back to get them."

Giggling in the background.

"Skip. Oh my god. Are you fucking Lola?"

"Jesus, Eve, what the hell? Where did that come from?"

"Why is she there?"

"I told you."

I lost it.

"Liar!" I shouted into the phone.

An elderly couple passing me on their way into the dining room jumped visibly. I hoped I hadn't given them heart attacks.

"Eve, listen, let me explain…"

"Explain what? That you're fucking the nanny? God, Skip, that's so trite."

"I think you mean cliche," Skip corrected.

"Are you fucking kidding me?"

"Look, I've been meaning to talk to you. I just didn't want to ruin your vacation with Tamara."

"Of course not," I said through my teeth. "And now we've talked. Good bye, Skip."

I ended the call before I could say something that made me feel more stupid than I already did. My husband and the nanny. Only Mia Farrow could feel worse.

Instinctively, I walked back into the restaurant, only to realize what a stupid move that was. There was no way I was having dinner in that place. Couples were everywhere, nuzzling, giggling. Only I was alone, wondering at the relationships I was observing. Man and wife? Man and mistress?

A tiny tube of lipstick and a fifty-second phone call. That was all it had taken for my world to finally unhinge.

Except, of course, that I knew that wasn't really true. I knew how very many drops had fallen into the bucket before it spilled over.

"Excuse me," I whispered, grabbing a waitress as she passed. "I'm wondering if you could help me. I'm dining alone tonight, and I...ah...don't think this is really the place for me. I just want somewhere I can tuck in with a book..."

My voice trailed off as the girl looked at me in sympathy. She nodded.

"There's The Runcible Spoon," she said.

"Toward Misquamicut," a voice interjected, startling me.

"I'm heading there now."

*Oh, Jesus H. Christ on a motorbike, it's the guy with the abs
and the nonchalance.*

"Hey, Finn," the waitress smiled.

"Hey, Shana. How's it going?"

He smiled absently back at her, then turned to me.

"I can give you a lift, or you can follow me. It's just a
few minutes away."

"I'm not sure Misquamicut is what I'm looking for
tonight," I said, thinking of the raucous bars I knew lined the
beach there.

"This is different. Close to the beach, but just far enough
off the beaten path. Very low key." He nodded at the novel
tucked under my arm. "You and your book will have a fine
time."

This was all so unexpected, I had no idea how to
respond. The waitress, Shana, bailed on me, leaving me with
Finn of the Rock-Hard Abs.

"Oh, ah...thank you," I said slowly. "All I need is the
address for my GPS."

Finn stepped back from me, leaned over the bar for a
moment, and then handed me a cocktail napkin with an address
scrawled on it. There was a phone number, too, but I didn't ask
if it was the restaurant's or his.

"Thank you," I said.

I turned and left as quickly as possible.

In the car, I paused before entering the address into the
GPS. Was this a good idea? This Finn had told me he would be

there. If I went there now, would he assume it indicated something beyond the desire for a decent, quiet meal in solitude?

Would he be right?

My face flushed.

"Stop," I told myself. "You're being ridiculous."

I pictured Finn as I'd seen him at the bar, gorgeous and self-assured. The kind of guy who dated models half his age. In other words, out of my league. I may have been The Red Fox in law school, but now I was just Mrs. Wolcott, and what did that mean? I was a stay-at-home mom whose boys were in boarding school. I was facing down the big four-oh while my husband screwed the nanny. I was a joke.

I felt tears welling up in my eyes and a lump rising in my throat as I put the car into gear. I reached the road and paused, thinking of how easy it would be to just turn around, let the valet take the car from me and think whatever he would as I slunk back to my cottage. I could polish off the cheese tray while I watched Law and Order reruns. I could go to bed early and be up in time for sunrise yoga on the beach.

"Oh, fuck it," I breathed.

I followed the GPS to The Runcible Spoon.

It was a tiny, quaint restaurant tucked between the beach and a dead-end street. I found Finn holding the door open for me.

"I was afraid you'd gotten lost," he said.

I blushed deeply.

"A little trouble starting out, but I made it. Thank you."

The hostess looked from me to Finn.

"Are you two...?" she asked, an eyebrows raised.

"Oh, no," I said. "Not together."

"Well, we could be," Finn offered. "I mean, if you like. I know you've got that book and all, but if you wanted some company?"

The hostess smirked.

"Two tables for one or one table for two?"

I had the sense she'd been practicing that line and waiting for an opportunity to use it.

"Well?" Finn asked.

The phone call – Skip and Lola and the insanity of my life – came back to me. I could be the jilted wife dining alone with a book, or I could have dinner with a hunky stranger.

"Table for two, then," I said.

"Inside or out?"

Finn and I looked at each other with raised eyebrows and simultaneously said, "Out?" We laughed while the hostess looked bemused.

She led us to a table in a secluded corner of the canopied deck, where the breeze lifted the white linen tablecloth ever-so-slightly and the sounds and smells of the beach drifted in like music. Hurricane jars held white candles all around, and I noticed the other diners sat at a distance. This was clearly the prime table for a romantic dinner. The hostess winked at me as she handed me my menu.

A waitress introduced herself and took our drink orders. I fumbled with the phone in my purse, checking to be sure the boys hadn't texted, then shutting the ringer off.

"Expecting an important message?" Finn asked.

"Oh, well, sort of," I said. "Kids. Just making sure my kids hadn't texted me."

"And you have...?"

"Two boys. Twelve and fourteen. They're at boarding school," I explained, "and I want to be sure they're settling in all right, but it seems boys that age have more important things to do than talk to their mother."

"Ah," Finn said, as if he simply could not relate.

"No kids?" I asked him.

He shook his head.

"Nope. I do have a cat, though. Oscar Wilde."

I laughed. The waitress brought our drinks, silencing our conversation for a moment.

"Cheers," Finn said, and we clinked glasses. I took a long sip of wine.

"So, you have a cat named Oscar Wilde," I said, still amused. "You've condemned a poor little kitty to die shamed and destitute and alone?"

"No, no," Finn laughed. "Times have changed. What goes on between my Oscar Wilde and the neighbor's tomcat is their business. He'll write himself a much happier ending than his namesake. He's bold and devil-may-care and he's found himself a good human."

Finn placed his phone on the table between us and displayed a picture. I picked up the phone for a closer look and let out a loud laugh. There was Finn on a stand-up paddle board, and there was a giant Maine coon cat - wearing a tiny yellow life vest - on the nose of the board.

"You're joking!" I cried, shaking my head. "Tell me this is Photoshopped."

"No way. He loves it," Finn insisted. "Well, except for the life jacket, but we had a scare off Napatree point one day. I tell you, you haven't lived until you've tried to pull a panicked cat out of the surf onto a paddle board. Nothing like claws ripping you to ribbons in the salt water. So I just told him, that's it. You wear the life vest or no more boarding."

"And he agreed to this?" I chuckled, taking another long sip of my wine. I could feel that pleasant buzz returning and reminded myself what that had led to at the spa earlier in the day. Mentally, I cautioned myself to slow down.

"Well, it's generally his way or the highway, so he must have consented, or you wouldn't be seeing that picture." Finn took a sip of his drink and grinned at me with that dead-sexy smile. "So, aside from the rug rats, do you have pets?"

I bristled slightly at the reference to my boys as "rug rats." I knew he meant to be funny, but this was Max and Eli he was talking about.

"We had a dog, Sally. She grew up with the kids. But then she had a tumor just about two years ago and we had to put her down."

"What kind of dog?" Finn asked, then he held up his hand. "No - wait! Let me guess." He ran his eyes up and down me, and I felt suddenly self-conscious. "Golden retriever."

"How'd you know?" I asked coolly.

"There's a type."

"Is there?"

I bristled again.

"Sure," he returned breezily. "Understated Talbots dress. Pearl earrings. Kids at boarding school. It was either a Golden or a chocolate lab."

I tried to ignore his assessment of me, of how neatly I could fit into a very ordinary box. I understood that only too well. In fact, I wasn't sure who I was more upset with at the moment: Finn or myself. I forced myself to smile at him widely.

"Actually," I said. "Sally was a Leonberger."

Finn looked slightly stunned.

"A....*what*?" he asked.

"A Leonberger," I repeated. "In the same family as the Great Pyrnees and Burnese Mountain Dogs. I'd read something about them as a kid and was fascinated. Then I was volunteering at the Animal Rescue League, and what comes in? A Leonberger. She was about a year old at the time, surrendered because she was barking incessantly. The manager and the director were looking at her, trying to figure out what she was. The owner thought she was a mix of shepherd and retriever, but I knew right away. I adopted her on the spot."

"And did you get her to stop barking?" Finn asked.

"Never," I laughed. "She probably took years off my life, all the times she'd start howling in the middle of the night. I'd be alone with the kids, and Sally'd start barking at three a.m. No reason, but at three a.m. your mind goes crazy places, like, 'there must be a serial killer just outside the bedroom door.' I can't tell you how many times I went tiptoeing through my house in the dark with a golf club."

"And where was your husband at three a.m.?" Finn asked, a hint of challenge in his question.

"Good question, right?" I said, trying to keep the edge out of my voice. "Honestly? We've spent most of our marriage apart. He's either in Boston for work while I'm in Jamestown with the kids, or he's in Miami with his mother while I'm taking the boys skiing…"

Or he's in my house fucking the nanny while I'm having dinner with you.

I bit my tongue and reached again for my wine glass.

With impeccable timing, the waitress arrived to take our dinner orders. In need of comfort food, I decided on the lobster roll, and while Finn ordered the same, as well as another round of drinks, I had just enough time to turn and dab at the corners of my eyes before my makeup ran.

Two hours and several drinks later, I was again dabbing at my eyes, but this time because I was hysterical with laughter.

"So wait," I said. "You peed on a midget?"

The waitress cleared the last of our dishes and left us with just a candle and our drinks on the table between us. I had the sense she was hoping we'd leave soon, as most of the other diners had cleared out while Finn and I talked and laughed.

"I think they prefer to be called 'little people'," Finn replied, deadpan.

"Does it matter when you're peeing on them?"

"Look, it wasn't like that was the plan," Finn clarified. "I just left the bar and relieved myself on this shrub. Then this little guy jumps up, yelling. How was I to know he was sleeping under there? I offered to make it up to him with a drink, but he just swore at me in Spanish and took off."

"And this was in Brazil?"

"Honduras. I could tell you the stories from Brazil, but then I'd have to kill you," Finn grinned.

I took another sip of my wine.

"And you go to all these places to do what, again?" I asked.

"Paraglide," Finn responded patiently, an amused smile on his lips.

"Which is like parasailing, but without the boat - right?" I attempted to clarify my limited understanding.

"Sort of. You travel on thermals. Rising hot air."

"What if there's no hot air?" I asked.

"That's why we choose our location and watch the weather carefully."

"So, it's dangerous?" Something about that thought appealed to me.

"Not if you know what you're doing. There are places where thermals happen. Ever see a bird just hovering over a bridge, kind of coasting? He's riding a thermal."

I looked at Finn and realized the wine might have begun to cloud my judgment. He looked as though he always knew what he was doing.

"I think I'm drunk," I said bluntly.

"You should probably stop drinking wine, then," Finn said, moving my half-empty glass away from me.

"What are you drinking?" I asked. I couldn't recall what he'd ordered, and I couldn't identify the beverage in the glass.

"Ketel One," he said. "With apple juice."

I laughed, probably a bit too loudly.

"You've paired good vodka with apple juice? Seriously?"

Finn nodded and took another sip.

"It's my landing drink. Concocted by accident. Jake, the paragliding buddy I told you about? He proposed a toast when we landed that day in Vermont, the time when we narrowly missed the cold front. He had Ketel One, but not much. I had apple juice in my Camelback. A couple of plastic cups, some teamwork, and voila!"

"And that tastes good?" I asked skeptically.

"Try it." He slid his glass toward me.

I shook my head.

"I don't think I should."

Finn laughed.

"Nothing's worse than that wine you're drinking. All sugar - makes for a nasty hangover. Here," he said, pushing a glass of water toward me.

I took a long drink.

"How'd you end up at Ocean Manor all alone?" he asked, catching me off guard.

"I have a friend," I said stupidly.

Fabulous. My mouth was speaking without the full cooperation of my brain.

"I mean, my friend Tamara, we do this every year, spend some time here. A girls' getaway - no husbands, no kids. But Nana – her grandmother – died today, so here I am. Alone." I giggled. "Well, except that I'm not alone *right now*, but you know that."

I took another long drink of water.

"Hey," I leveled my gaze at him. "So what do you do for work that leaves you free to zip all over the globe paragliding and whatever? I mean, you do work, right?"

"Not much anymore. I guess you could say I'm retired."

"Retired? But how old are you?"

"Forty-two."

"How does one retire at forty-two?" I asked, genuinely intrigued.

"Well, I'm an architect by trade," he explained. "A while back, I had this idea that the right software could make a couple of difficult aspects of my job easier, but I couldn't find anything on the market that fit my needs. So I invented a program. Turned out, it fit not only my needs, but the needs of just about every practicing architect out there. Microsoft bought it." He shrugged. "I went on vacation and decided I liked that better than work. Now I don't work unless the project really grabs me."

"You just don't work," I laughed.

"Not unless I want to," Finn said. "And if I really don't want to, I don't have to, not ever again. But sometimes a project just seems right, so then I work. It's a balance thing."

"It sounds like you have the perfect balance."

"I think I do. But hey - your turn," he said. "I saw that car of yours. How did *you* make all of *your* money?"

I felt something catch in my throat. I tipped my head toward the ceiling and reached again for my wine glass, swirling the liquid as I brought it to my lips.

"The good old-fashioned way," I said at last, looking somewhere over his head. "I married well."

Silence from across the table made me drop my gaze. When I looked up, I found Finn focused on me intently.

"Nah," he said. "You're too smart for that."

I had to look away again. I thought of my parents' hopes for me, my own expectations, and the myriad ways I'd failed in each capacity.

I laughed and shook my head.

"You give me too much credit," I said, working to keep a teasing lilt in my voice. "But enough about me. Or even about you, and your architect-and-computer stuff. Aside from paragliding, what does one do when one is 'retired' at age forty-two?"

Finn gave me a devious grin.

"Whatever the hell one wants."

I laughed again, a little too loudly, and I realized I'd

definitely had too much to drink. I set my glass down. Finn motioned for the waitress to refill my water glass and pushed it toward me again.

"Seriously," he said, "It feels good to be free. Until the Microsoft thing sort of fell in my lap, I'd always assumed there were just these things I *had* to do, no choice. But now? It's all choice. I can do whatever I want to do."

"That must be nice," I said, rolling my eyes.

"What's keeping you from doing whatever you want to do?" Finn challenged.

"Oh, I don't know," I mused mockingly. "A husband, two kids, three houses and an absolute *shitload* of volunteer and social obligations. Oh, and the mother-in-law from hell."

"That's a whole mess of anchors," Finn agreed, but I somehow felt he was making fun of me. "You should probably hang onto the kids, but what about the rest of it? Couldn't you clear your calendar? And how bad could the mother-in-law be?"

"How bad?" I laughed. "She's the devil in Lily Pulitzer."

"Ouch," Finn said, clearly amused. "Go on…"

I clicked my tongue against my teeth as I searched for the right words. How to describe Kitty Wolcott?

She stood six feet tall even at the age of eighty-eight. She was frighteningly thin, as blue-blooded women of her generation tended to be, so that her expensive clothing always hung from her at painfully acute angles. Her eyes were slanted from a decades-ago facelift, yet loose skin draped in folds about her chin that called to mind the jowls of a malnourished dog, or perhaps a really goddamned ugly turkey. Her hair was a cut, color and style reminiscent of Cruella DeVille, a sharp contrast study in black and white that seemed deliberately intended to invoke severity and inspire fear. She kept her nails long, filed to a point and glazed with clear polish that yellowed and left them looking like claws at the ends of her long fingers.

But the aspect of Kitty I had always found most disconcerting was the proliferation of moles over every area of skin visible to the eye. They were everywhere. Tamara had dubbed her, "Holy Moley," and rightly so. For the life of me, I could never fathom how a woman with so damn much money allowed herself to be overrun by dark, ugly moles. Unless, of course, that was the point. To prove she was so damn rich and important she just didn't give a shit what she looked like. It might even have been a deliberate distraction, or a test of some sort. Heaven knew, it was all I could do when speaking with Kitty not to be completely distracted by all the moles bobbing about. I've imagined it's only a matter of time before I involuntarily let loose a stream of verbal venom directed at those nasty moles and the nastier woman hosting them.

I tried to explain all this to Finn without reducing Kitty to a caricature, but the more I explained, the harder Finn and I both laughed.

"And she lives right near you?" he asked.

"In Newport," I explained. "We've got the East Passage separating us from her, but I think I need a larger body of water. The Atlantic, say."

"Well, she's eighty-eight. She'll kick the bucket soon. Or..." Finn mimed giving an invisible person a shove "...maybe have an unfortunate accident at the yacht club. Mother-in-law problem solved. Now, how about the husband, because I've got to be honest: you seem awfully flirtatious for a happily married woman."

"I'm not!" I protested.

"Not happily married?"

"Not flirtatious," I corrected him, but then I laughed, "or happily married. I am neither. But to be clear, you're the flirt here. I am just the pathetic woman whose husband is home screwing the nanny."

"Really?" Finn's eyes widened. "That's so cliche."

"Not trite?"

"What?"

"Never mind."

I reached past the water and polished off the last of my drink.

"You know what I hear is the perfect cure for that sort of situation?" he asked coyly.

I played along.

"Revenge sex with a handsome stranger?"

Finn blinked, clearly surprised. Which made two of us; good God, how much wine had I drunk to become this bold? Then that slow, sexy smile of his stole back across his face.

"I was going to say a day of paddle boarding and maybe a surf lesson," he said, "but whatever you prefer."

We left the restaurant and strolled along the beach. The cool sand between my toes felt heavenly, but the most unwelcome thought popped into my mind. *I am thirty-nine years old, and I have never before done anything this bold or potentially stupid.* I wasn't sure which bothered me more: the idea of how safe and sheltered my life had always been, or the notion that I'd wandered off onto a dark beach with a man I didn't really know. When some fisherman found my shark-nibbled remains off Montauk, Dateline would profile me as the idiot whore who'd gotten herself killed by lust, tragically abandoning her husband and sons. I could just see some decade-old family snapshot where they'd pan in on my smiling face, could hear the solemn voice-over, *"But what Eve didn't know about the handsome stranger who called himself Finn Berwick would cost her her life."*

"Gorgeous night, huh?" Finn whispered in my ear as we walked, drawing me to him.

"My thought exactly," I lied. "So is this what you do here in Watch Hill? Find unhappily-married women and lure them out to the beach?"

"Yes, of course." Finn stopped, sheltering us in the hollow of a dune. His hands went to my hips, and he leaned in so his nose touched mine. "A different desperate housewife every weekend."

I wondered if this was one of those truths said in jest.

45

What if this really was his game, preying on sorry women with sorrier marriages?

What if I didn't care?

"I would like to kiss you," Finn said, his voice so soft I almost missed it over the sound of the surf.

"I think you should," my voice replied, and then his arms were around me, his mouth on mine.

There was enough alcohol in my blood to make me feel deliciously lightheaded, but was there enough that I could ever claim – truthfully – that the devil in the bottle made me do it? My head was spinning, but oddly enough, the thoughts seemed to come to me in slow-motion. Finn was kissing me, and I felt his mouth, his tongue, on what seemed a molecular level. *Dammnit, Eve. It's a kiss. Just a kiss.* How was I feeling it as I did? At every contact point within and around my mouth. In the gentle but firm press of his palm against my spine. Through the tips of his fingers at my jawbone, my temples, tangled in my hair. And in those places he hadn't touched, not yet: inside my thighs, between my legs.

Did Skip ever kiss me like this? Had it just been too long?

Oh shit, Skip.

My husband.

What the hell am I doing?

My brain (my goddamned, nuisance brain) kicked in and I felt the flames in my thighs begin to die down. I quickly conjured an image of Skip with that backstabbing Lola, but I was too smart for myself. I knew what I was trying to do, and I wouldn't be guiltless, no matter how I tried. Just because Skip didn't give a shit about our vows didn't mean I was free of my promises. It was a matter of character. Skip was just Skip. He couldn't help himself. Right?

Shit, now I was channeling Kitty. *Some men are just that way. Boys will be boys.* Shit. *Bullshit.*

I'd never been this confused in my life. I'd never wanted so badly to just *be bad* for a change, to just do the wrong thing because it felt right in the moment. To pretend I was someone else, that I'd done things differently in my life. That I could have passion instead of responsibility.

"Where are you, Eve?" Finn whispered, his lips brushing my ear and then nibbling, just the tiniest bit.

The flames rose again. Fireworks went off. Use whatever hackneyed spontaneous combustion metaphor you like, and that was me, lost.

"Right here," I murmured, and it was true. I was back. I felt Finn's mouth on mine, my toes in the sand, every grain awakening nerve endings, and then his toes as they found my instep, my ankle, my calf. Before I knew it he had maneuvered - deftly, like a dancer - so that my left leg rose, lightly, until my heel was in the small of his back. Thanks to the spur-of-the-moment Brazilian, I felt the sea breeze through the thin fabric of my panties so fully that the night air seemed a force all its own. I was suddenly aware of just how exposed I was, and all this right out in the open. The restaurant we'd abandoned was close enough that I could hear laughter and the clink of glasses drifting out on the salt air, but far enough away that I again considered the foolishness of my position. I was out on the beach with a virtual stranger.

"Finn," I whispered, trying to form the beginnings of a protest.

He stopped and tipped his head at me, drawing back just enough that I could see the sparkle of his dark eyes in the moonlight. Unspoken, the question passed between us. Stop or go? I thought of all the reasons I should stop, some more obvious than others.

I was married.

With children.

And Finn was clearly a womanizer.

He'd taken me from shy-and-inhibited to hey-that's-my-leg-wrapped-around-his-waist in no time.

That was bad.

Very bad.

I should have apologized and left, made my way back to my car, back to Ocean Manor.

Instead, my hand cupped the back of his head and I drew him to me. His mouth closed over mine again, and I melted. There was nothing forceful about his actions, and yet I felt as though I had no choice, that something primal inside me had risen up and outvoted my common sense. I was answering some call that had too long lain silent deep within me. A wave crashed on the beach, and my heart beat loudly. That was it: cheesy as it sounds, I felt carried on a tide. I couldn't have stopped if I tried.

As if confirming my thoughts, Finn let out a low,

guttural sound, leaning against me. *Holy shit, he was hard as a rock.* In a single, swift movement, he swept my panties aside and I felt his hand between my legs. Skin on skin, his fingers setting me on fire.

Yep.

His fingers.

Inside my panties.

This guy I'd known about three and a half hours.

Not my husband, by the way.

I gasped and pulled away from him, away from the animal thing inside myself. I shivered, but I suspected it was Sensible Eve's death throes. I turned and ran down the path through the dunes and teetered at the water's edge. A wave lapped at my toes, the water surprisingly warm in the cool of the evening.

I heard Finn behind me. He stopped short, giving me space, but I could still feel the heat of his body.

"Eve? I'm sorry. Are you okay?"

The thought came to me from thin air. What was Skip doing right now? I wanted to picture him alone at home, maybe looking out over the water at the very same moon that loomed large over me just then, teary-eyed as he contemplated calling me. I wanted to think he was counting his faults, the ways he had wronged me, and planning to find some way to make it all right. I wanted to believe he really cared that he'd hurt me, that he understood at last that he'd hurt me over and over and over again, but the truth was, I just couldn't picture it.

I could picture him screwing Lola in my pool at my

house.

I could picture him drinking and shouting with his brothers in a bar in Newport, buying drinks for groups of sparkly-attired women half their age.

I could even picture him with a glass of Scotch and porn on the big screen in our living room.

I just couldn't picture him thinking of me.

For a sharp, bright moment I felt focused and clear, as clear as I hadn't felt in years. The moonlight shone down from above, illuminating a path on the dark water below. It was almost as though I could walk on that path clear across the water, and find a better life waiting for me up ahead. Or I could dive in, immerse myself in the alien world of the sea. I could become a mermaid and swim away from it all. A smile spread slowly across my face.

As I had all my life, I wondered about the creatures in the depths of the sea. Were there whales out there right now? Sharks? While I stood there, toes at the water's edge, caught between my real life and this fantasy I'd dropped into, there was a whole other world out there, teeming with life, just beneath the placid surface. The thought of it thrilled me and left me lost in wonder.

Roughly, I took my left hand in my right. I ripped my wedding and engagement rings from my fingers, scraping the knuckle they hadn't passed in ages. I held them in my palm, and I could almost have sworn the moonlight hit them deliberately, making them sparkle. I thought of all they once meant to me, how sheltered and loved I'd felt just seeing them there on my hand, knowing that Skip had chosen me – *me!* – for all time. How small they looked now. How dull and insignificant.

"Wait..." Finn whispered, just inches behind me. His voice was taut with an apprehension I could feel in my belly.

I pretended not to hear him. It was like that moment of balancing on the edge of a dock, trying to summon the courage for a plunge into the chilly ocean. *Will I? Won't I?*

I hauled back and flung my rings into the surf.

Goodbye, Eve and Skip, mousy girl and golden boy!

Farewell, Eve the obedient!

Rest in peace, happily-ever-after!

So long!

Good riddance!

I almost felt as if this simple, symbolic (and, frankly, fiscally stupid) move had changed me. Freed me. Somewhere out there, a bluefish was sucking down fifty grand worth of diamonds and platinum. And all I felt was *alive*.

I closed the space between Finn and myself in two paces. I grabbed his lovely linen shirt there where it was open at the collar, feeling the muscles of his chest give way to his remarkable abs as I dragged downward, tearing through the buttons until they were gone. I hooked my hand over the fly of his jeans, feeling my fingertips graze his erection. I pulled him against me, startling myself with my strength as our pelvic bones collided. I was not myself, and I was loving it.

"Fuck me," I whispered, looping my tongue around Finn's ear lobe. "Hard."

Happily, he took instruction well.

51

Finn scooped me up and carried me into the relative shelter of the dunes. He spread his ruined linen shirt beneath me. Apparently chivalry was not dead. He fumbled in his pocket for a condom. In a frenzy of motion, my dress ended up somewhere around my ears, my panties were lost entirely, and Finn's tongue was on, over, and inside me so deftly that I came before I even had time to enjoy it. When – *oh when?!* – was the last time I'd had an orgasm that didn't happen alone, clandestinely, in my bathroom? I clutched at him, pulling him inside me while I was still tingling, and though his attempt at restraint was admirable, it was all over in a matter of seconds. I lay there, gazing up at a sky so shrouded with clouds that no stars shone through, and waited for my nerves to stop singing.

The heat of the moment gave way to the cool of the evening, and I shivered, tugging my dress down around me. Finn wriggled back into his jeans and gathered me up in his arms. We lay there and I listened to our breathing. I'd leapt from the precipice. There was no going back. I had thrown away something broken, and I'd done something hopelessly reckless. Something indefensible. I thought about that as we lay there, and I wondered why I was not feeling panicked. Why I was not feeling guilty. Why, if asked, I would only have described how I felt in the moment as *free*.

"I was going to impress you with my knowledge of astronomy," Finn said evenly, his eyes on the cloudy sky above, "but Mother Nature isn't cooperating."

I laughed.

"I think you've impressed me enough for one night, Mr.

Berwick."

"Really?" he teased, suddenly energized enough to straddle me. He pinned my hips to the ground, the heat from his groin seeping into me. He took my wrists in his right hand, raising them over my head, while he leaned in to kiss me. I tried to imagine how his body would look in daylight. Right now, in the moonlight, his torso was killing me. Muscle and sweat and the lines of his tattoos. He was like a creature from another planet. Given time, I suspected he could be an endless source of fascination to me.

"*Really*," I taunted.

As it turned out, he was able to impress me further.

Chapter **Three**

Sunlight stung my eyes as I blinked them open. It took me a moment to make sense of where I was. A breeze stirred white curtains in the open window, and the sound of waves lapping at the shore came to my ears. Ocean Manor. I was back in my suite at Ocean Manor. I sat up in bed slowly. Christ, my head was pounding.

A half-finished bottle of Gatorade sat on the bedside table, a bottle of ibuprofen beside it. I washed down three of the pills with a swallow of Gatorade, and then I remembered.

Finn Berwick. Dinner and drinks. And more drinks. And then...

I exhaled and sank back into the pillows. I brought my hands to my face and saw the naked white indentation where my wedding and engagement rings should have been. I'd really done it, hadn't I? I'd chucked my rings into the ocean and screwed a complete stranger on the beach.

Classy.

"Who *are* you?" I asked myself aloud.

As if in answer, I heard a key in the lock, and the suite door began to open.

Oh god, had I brought him back here? Had I given him a key?

"Holy fuck, thank god! You're alive!"

"Tam?"

I nearly wept with joy (and maybe a little bit of relief) as my best friend burst into the room. She was her usual eclectic self, radiating energy from head to toe. Her super-short hair shot out from her head in artfully-mussed platinum spikes. Long silver earrings in the shape of arrows dangled against her face. Her toned, tanned legs went on forever beneath a brightly flowered minidress. And though it had to be nearly eighty degrees outside, she had her favorite well-worn Frye boots on her feet. She crossed the room and kissed the top of my head, then picked up the phone and the iPhone from the bedside table and waved them at me.

"These are called phones, Eve," she scolded me. "When they make that ringing noise, you answer them. That way your best friend doesn't think you fucking died or something."

I smiled and nodded silently. Tamara stepped back and took a good look at me.

"Holy shit, it's nearly noon and you're still in bed. You've got the telltale Gatorade and Advil by the bed, and frankly, you look like ass. This is some very un-Eve-like behavior. You've got some 'splainin' to do."

"Oh, you have no idea," I moaned. I leapt suddenly from the bed and lurched toward the bathroom. "I think I'm going to be sick."

Tamara followed me into the bathroom and held my hair while I hung inelegantly over the toilet bowl, dry heaving. Nothing came up. I stood slowly, looking down at my nightshirt, and realized I couldn't remember changing and getting into bed the night before. I couldn't even remember getting back to the hotel. I returned to the bed and flopped down onto my back with a sigh.

"Holy shit," Tamara laughed. "When I sent you to the spa I didn't think you'd come back with a pussy that looks like a naked mole rat."

"Hey!" I cried, sitting up and tugging my nightshirt down. "If you must know," I pouted, "I think that was the start of the trouble. Which makes it all your fault."

"Only the start? Who are you and what have you done with my best friend?"

The knock at the door silenced both of us. We looked at each other.

"Housekeeping?" Tamara guessed.

"Come back later," I called.

"No can do," came the response, a deep male voice.

Oh shit. *Finn.*

Tamara gave me a look, then pounced on the door. She swung it open wide, and there indeed stood Finn, every bit as tall and fabulous-looking as my limited memory allowed me to recall. He wore khaki shorts and a navy tee shirt that clung to his chiseled midsection. Tattoos ran down his arms. He was holding a large Thermos and a box of doughnuts. I tugged at my nightshirt and tucked myself under the bed sheet, then ran a hand hopelessly through my hair. Tamara had already told me I looked like ass, and now here was this painfully hot guy to witness it. Perfect.

"Hey," he said to me, glancing through the open French doors into the bedroom as he crossed to the kitchenette. "I figured you might need my hangover cure."

He set down the Thermos and opened the box. While Tamara stared, he put the doughnuts onto a plate and poured drinks into three glasses.

"Oh, sorry," he said, walking to Tamara and handing her a glass. He extended his hand toward her free one. "I'm Finn."

"Tamara," she said, still staring.

"I tried calling," Finn said to me, "but it went straight to voice mail."

"Oh," was all I could think to say.

I felt paralyzed. I still had not quite fully processed what I'd done the night before, and now here I sat, brutally hung over, watching worlds collide.

Finn brought me a drink and set the plate of doughnuts down on the bed.

"These are the good ones," he said, nodding at the plate. "They'll sit in your stomach for a week before they digest. Just what you need right now."

He brought a drink over for himself and sat on the edge of the bed next to me. Tamara still stood in the middle of the doorway, drink in hand, gaping.

"As my grandfather used to say, it's not the drinking that hurts. It's the stopping." Finn raised his glass. "Cheers!"

I was dumbstruck. He was so casual, so comfortable. He'd made himself right at home in my hotel room.

"Drink up," he said, then tipped his head me. "You all right?"

"It's just," I started, unsure of what to say. "I sort of assumed I wouldn't see you again."

He grinned.

"Ah, so that's your game. Love 'em and leave 'em."

"I sort of assumed it was yours," I countered.

Tamara slowly took a seat, still in the next room but positioned with a perfect view of the bedroom through the French doors. She took a sip of her drink. She looked like she was watching a show. Which, I suppose, she pretty much was.

"I had a great time last night," Finn said. "At dinner," he added, as if to clarify, then added with a wink, "Well, and after, too. I was hoping you might be free for dinner tonight." He seemed to remember Tamara. He looked her way and said, "But maybe you have plans?"

"Oh no," Tamara said. "I've gotta be home for dinner. Make-your-own pizza night. The kids'd burn down the house with Howard's level of supervision."

Thanks, Tam. Way to be a pal.

I drew a deep breath and wondered if this would be any easier if my head wasn't pounding.

"I don't think..." I began. "I mean, listen." I lowered my voice and looked apologetically at Finn. "I don't usually do *that*. I mean, not just not usually. Never. Ever. Not in my whole life. So, I'm sorry if I gave you the wrong idea. I mean, I *know* I gave you the wrong idea. I just...can't."

Finn smiled. He reached for the notepad and pen on the bedside table. He scrawled a number, then put the pen down. He held the slip of paper in front of me.

"Call me," he said as I took it. He stood, leaning in to kiss my cheek lightly. "Just dinner. Seven-ish?"

I watched him leave, thinking oh-so-inappropriately that his ass looked just as good in khaki shorts as it did in jeans. He closed the suite door behind him and Tamara emerged from her trance.

"Holy. Flying. Fuck." She stood and looked at me pointedly, shaking her head. "I leave you alone in a hotel for one evening, and you let the body-snatchers get you." She paused, apparently considering the possible double entendre in her words. "Well, *yeah*." She crossed the room and tapped the bedside clock. "Come on. I reserved a cabana. Drink up and get your bathing suit on. You, Eve Wolcott, are gonna nurse your hangover beachside and do some serious dishing."

Three hours later, my head was still throbbing, but less intensely. I was on my second Bloody Mary, and I'd been sipping water incessantly. Tamara had dragged me into the chilly waves for a swim, and I felt almost human again. She'd also elicited from me the entire sordid story of the previous night - or at least, as much of it as I could remember properly. She just kept shaking her head and saying things like, "No fucking way," and "I guess it *is* always the quiet ones."

"Seriously, Tam," I said, lying back on my lounge chair and adjusting my sunglasses. "I behaved so badly I could've been you."

"Oh, sweetheart," she said. "I never thought I'd hear myself say this, but I think you may finally have me beat." She took a sip of her drink, a virgin daiquiri since she would be driving home shortly. "So, you gonna call Adam Levine and take him up on his dinner offer?"

"Adam Levine?" I asked. "You mean Finn?"

"Duh."

"Who's Adam Levine?"

"Seriously?" Tamara wrinkled her nose at me. "Honestly, Eve, do you live under a rock? I'm gonna get you a subscription to *People* magazine for Christmas. All pop culture references seem to elude you. Adam Levine. Hunky, heavily tattooed and majorly fuckable Maroon Five frontman?"

"Maroon Five?"

"Judge on The Voice?"

I shook my head at her.

"Google him," she said. "When you've got time to spare and a vibrator handy. Your fuckbuddy Finn could be his brother."

"Shhhhh!" I hissed. In a whisper, I said, "He's not my fuckbuddy. He's not my anything. I did something bad. Something stupid. Something very stupid and very bad. I'm not going to have dinner with him. I'm not going to talk to him, even. Not ever again."

"Jeez, Evie, settle down."

"Listen, Tam, I've got a real problem, and it's that my marriage is over."

I dropped my head and bit at the edges of my thumbnail. Two small boys ran past our cabana, fighting over a sand pail. I was reminded of my boys. In some ways, it seemed they'd been that age just yesterday, but in others it seemed like a different lifetime. Instinctively, I picked up my iPhone and swiped it open. No texts from Eli or Max.

"You're really done?"

I waited for Tamara to say something snarky. She'd never liked Skip, not even the slightest little bit.

"Done," I affirmed. "I shouldn't have complicated things further, doing…well, what I did with Finn last night. But that's beside the point, really. How many different ways have I tried to make it work with Skip? How many times have I forgiven him for…" My voice trailed off.

"For compulsively dropping trou and sticking his dick into other women?" Tamara finished for me.

"Right. How many years have I been the person he and his family expected me to be, instead of who I really am? And how do I even know who I really am anymore? For the past decade, I've been on so many antidepressants and anti-anxiety meds, I feel like a lab rat." I pressed my forehead into my hands. "I snapped, Tam. That's what happened last night. I could feel it. Something inside me just…broke. I wanted to do the worst possible thing I could think to do. I wanted to crawl out of my skin, be anybody but myself. It had nothing to do with Finn, really. It could have been anyone. I just needed, for one evening, to be nothing like the good, obedient girl Skip has always assumed I am."

A wry smile tugged at one corner of Tamara's mouth.

"Well, then, you better just thank your lucky stars that the gods put Finn in your path," she said, tipping her head. "It could have been that guy."

I looked in the direction she'd indicated and dissolved into laughter. The hairiest man I'd ever seen, with a gold chain around his neck and a paunch hanging over the world's smallest Speedo, was strutting by, the wind teasing his comb-over into an alarming replica of a mohawk.

"Oh, Tam," I cried, "what would I do without you?"

She let a dismissive puff of air pass from her lips.

"Apparently, you'd fuck the bejeezus out of some random hot guy," she smirked. "Just sayin'."

She looked at her phone for the time and began gathering up her things.

"I hate to end a party with the new-and-improved Eve Wolcott, but I've gotta get back to the boys," she said. "I'm hoping to get the kiddos into bed early so I can fuck Howard on the kitchen table. All your tawdry tales have left me horny."

"How is Howard?" I asked as we walked back to the hotel. "How's his work?"

"Howard is batshit crazy, thank you for asking" Tamara said. "He's working on some installment piece for a new bar called 'Fluid,' and somehow this involves saving his urine in jars, a la Howard Hughes."

I winced.

"He's not going to work the urine into his sculpture somehow?" I asked hopefully. "I don't think I could drink in a bar with art featuring urine."

Tamara shrugged.

"Who knows? Ever since that fiasco where that little Damian Hirst wannabe outsold him at auction, he's been getting crazier and crazier. He calls it artistic license, but I think it's just a pissing contest." She stopped walking and raised her eyebrows comically. "If you'll pardon the pun."

I unlocked the door to the suite that should have been ours and realized I didn't want to stay there without Tamara.

"I'm gonna go home," I told her as we dropped our beach bags on the floor. "It's no fun here without you."

"Need I remind you of last night?" Tamara teased.

I punched her arm.

"Stop already. That was a mistake. A colossal mistake. It won't happen again." I sighed. "I'll go home and tell Skip I want a divorce, talk to Wally and get the name of an attorney, go from there. I'm not really in 'vacation' mode."

"Wait!" Tamara said, holding up her index finger.

She went into the bedroom, dropped her iPod into the dock on the bureau, and began scrolling through songs.

Cake's rendition of *I Will Survive*.

"Nope," she said.

Greg Kihn's *The Breakup Song*.

"Uh-uh."

Then Paul Simon came through the speakers. *Fifty Ways to Leave Your Lover.*

Tamara looked inspired. She began dancing around the room, loudly singing along with the song. Only she replaced the word "lover" with "husband."

"Just slip out the back, Jack," she sang, grabbing me by the hands and making me dance along with her. "Go and fuck Steve, Eve…"

I laughed in spite of myself.

"There must be fifty ways to leave your husband!" I hollered.

Tamara and I collapsed on the bed, laughing like it was 1989 and this was a slumber party.

"Hey," I said to her once we calmed down. We lay side by side on the bed, watching the ceiling fan make lazy circles above us. An Aimee Mann tune had replaced Paul Simon on the iPod. The entire moment reminded me of college. "How are you doing with the Nana stuff?"

She looked taken aback. She waved a hand at me dismissively.

"Oh. Fine. Like I said, she was older than god and had things pretty well in order. Not a lot to do, really."

"That's not what I meant," I said, though I knew she understood.

"Yeah. Well, I hid in the shower for about twenty minutes crying yesterday, if that's what you mean." She let out a long sigh. "I just don't get it. Death, I mean. Makes no fucking sense. You're here one minute and then, *poof!* There's this shell you leave behind, but it doesn't even look like you anymore, not really. Where do you go? The real you, I mean - where the fuck is it? And why is it that it doesn't seem to matter if you're here ten years or ninety? The people you loved still feel like they've had their guts ripped out and shit on, either way."

"I'm sorry," I said, reaching out to wipe away a tear that had slipped down Tamara's cheek. "I loved her, and I love you, and you're right - there's never a good time for someone to die."

Tamara sniffed and rubbed at her eyes.

"Shit, Eve, I know no one understands that like you do."

I suddenly wished I hadn't steered us onto this subject.

"When will Nate and Ian arrive?" I asked.

"Tomorrow," Tamara said. "If it's too rocky at your house, come stay with us. Nate would be over the moon."

I smiled thinking of Nate. I'd long ago adopted Tamara's brother as my own. He was one of my very favorite people on the planet, and thankfully Ian, his partner of five-plus years, seemed every bit the great guy Nate deserved. A bit quiet, but that made him a good foil to Tamara's loud family. Two years ago, I'd taken the boys out to visit them in San Francisco, and it had been one of the best vacations I could recall.

"Be careful what you offer," I said. "That sounds pretty good."

Tamara bustled around the room, grabbing her iPod and bag. She pulled her boots back on and propped her sunglasses atop her head.

"You've always got a place with me, babe," she said.

She kissed me lightly on the tip of my nose, and then she was gone.

I decided to stay the night.

I'd called my home number and gotten no answer. I'd called Skip's cell and it had gone straight to voice mail. No good could come of driving to Jamestown to see what was preventing him from answering the phone.

I managed to get Eli on his phone, and he corralled Max for about thirty seconds of FaceTime. My baby was settling in at Morefield so well, I was already dispensable. Eli didn't seem to be doing as well, but he made it clear he didn't want to chat. I elicited a promise from him to call the next day, then I let him go.

I slipped into my night shirt and ordered room service. The tray was delivered by Caleb, who winked suggestively at my attire.

"I think you have something in your eye," I said blandly, handing him his tip and closing the door on him.

I plopped the tray on the bed and grabbed the TV remote. I considered my movie options.

A Walk to Remember.

Titanic.

The Notebook.

Clearly someone was trying to kill me.

At last I found one that wasn't a tear-jerker: *Dolores Claiborne.* Good old Stephen King. Perfect! I was in the mood for a movie about a woman who kills her husband.

"An accident, Dolores, can be an unhappy woman's best friend," said the woman onscreen.

"Amen," I said, raising my glass.

I briefly pictured Skip floating lifeless in our swimming pool, then shook my head. What the hell was wrong with me? I lay back on the bed and watched the movie, picking at my reasonably-good-for-room-service margherita pizza.

My phone buzzed with a text. I swept the screen and realized I'd missed several messages over the course of the evening, all from the same unfamiliar number.

At six-thirty: *Dinner?*

At seven: *Pretty please?*

At seven-thirty: *Am I being stood up?*

At eight-fifteen: *I'm making a nuisance of myself, aren't I?*

At nine-thirty: *Well, now I just feel pathetic.*

And just then, at nine-thirty-five: *Night, Eve.*

Oh, *Finn*, I thought. Just take your sexy self and move on. Stop reminding me of my very, very bad behavior.

I put the phone on the charger in the other room, then I went to brush my teeth and take my vitamins and meds. I stood in the pristine hotel bathroom trying not to feel the sadness that swirled in my belly like an impending storm. I looked at the row of bottles and tried to recall when I had last lived without drugs to help me feel sane.

My pregnancy with Max.

That was the last time I'd been drug-free.

Nearly thirteen years ago.

Since then, it had taken a never-ending series of medications and counselors to make me feel my life was tolerable. And why? I had everything I could ever want, didn't I? I had two beautiful children and more material wealth than most. My issues with Skip aside, I had it good, and I knew I had it good, which ironically only made me feel that much more miserable. What ungrateful sort of person had all the blessings I had and needed pills to get by?

I looked at my reflection in the mirror. Red hair in the same shoulder-length style I'd kept it in for a decade. High cheekbones and a nose bridged with a smattering of freckles. Blue-green eyes framed lightly with laugh lines. I was still pretty, still could pass for a few years younger than the thirty-nine I had under my belt. But I wasn't getting any younger, and no one lives forever. Morbidly, I thought of my parents. If I followed the precedent they'd set, I had no more than twelve years left, maybe as little as two.

I opened the first bottle and took my multivitamin.

Then I looked at the other bottles and swept them into the trash.

Chapter **Four**

I didn't sleep.

I tossed and turned on those lovely Ocean Manor sheets, my mind racing. I'd start to doze off and find myself entangled in the strangest dreams, like a hall of mirrors encompassing my life, but with half the glass shattered. It was nightmarish and dangerous. Skip, Eli, Max, Kitty, Tamara, Finn – they all made appearances, each chiding me for my foolish behavior. Worse, I recalled my parents' deaths. My father at age forty-one and my mother at fifty-three. Both so young I had no ability to make sense of it. My mind ran on a punishing loop. So I'd sit up, turn on the light and power up my iPad, and scroll through nonsense until I felt sleepy again. By three a.m. I understood how sleep deprivation could be a powerful torture tactic. I'd have given anything to anyone just to be able to slip deeply into sleep for a few hours.

When the sky behind the curtains began to brighten, I dragged myself heavily from bed and went out onto the balcony to watch the sun rise. The air was chilly and I pulled my bathrobe tightly about me. This was the kind of morning where the smell of impending autumn was inescapable and bittersweet. It was cool and smoky, the salt air carrying the scent of falling leaves and blooming chrysanthemums. I touched the railing, then recoiled from the dampness of the morning dew. I wiped my hands on my bathrobe and watched the sun grow, lifting itself over the horizon, its orange warmth breaking the chill. There was little wind, and the waves shifted lazily beneath the growing light, the stain of orange a ripple on the surface. I felt suddenly lonelier than I'd ever been before. I stood there, swaying slightly in my fatigue, before turning my back on the impressive vista and retreating to my bed. I had to sleep. I simply had to.

And I did. After the longest night I could recall, sleep came at last. My dreams were still twisted and awful, but I slept. When I woke to a knock at the door, it was housekeeping.

"Come back later," I called.

I raised myself up enough to look at my phone. It was eleven a.m., and I'd missed three texts from Finn.

Nine o'clock: *Good morning, Eve.*

Nine-fifteen: *See how difficult I am to be rid of?*

Nine forty-five: *Breakfast? My treat...*

Ten-ten: *Clearly you think I am a gigantic asshole. I would like to prove I am not. Just call?*

Ten forty-five: *Jumping off bridge. All your fault.*

I laughed and shook my head in awe. What was with this guy?

And then there was another knock on the door. Not

housekeeping this time. Room service.

I sleepily stumbled to the door and opened it to find my buddy Caleb waiting with a cart. A bouquet of pale pink peonies sat beautifully amidst the covered dishes.

"I'm sorry," I said, raking a hand through the hair that fell over my eyes. "I didn't order room service."

"I did," Finn said, emerging from around the corner.

I glared accusingly at Caleb, who shrugged.

"Sorry," he said. "He tips better than you do."

I laughed and bit my lip, stepping aside to allow Caleb to enter. He arranged the food and flowers on the table in the dining area while Finn and I regarded each other awkwardly from either side of the doorway. When Caleb ducked back out, Finn stepped in.

"May I?" he asked.

"There doesn't seem to be any stopping you," I said, a bit more harshly than I'd intended.

"You're unhappy with me," Finn observed, but that thin, sexy smile stayed at the corners of his lips.

"Well, I don't generally entertain like this," I responded, indicating my bed-head and nightshirt.

Finn stepped in and put an end to our awkward standoff. He put his hands to my head, mussing my hair further. He kissed me gently, lightly nipping my lower lip. His hands slid slowly along my body, meandering from my head to my hips, and he drew me in close. It felt too familiar and too damn good all at once.

"I like you like this," he murmured, burying his lips in

my neck. "Like you've just been rolling around in bed. An appealing idea."

I wanted to tell him to knock it off, but the truth was, I was transfixed. I'd forgotten that new-romance feeling, the way the mere proximity or scent or sound of someone could weaken the knees as fully as any romance novel might suggest. It was intoxicating.

And then my mind went briefly where it shouldn't have: to Skip and his infidelities. I had an unwanted flash of understanding. This was what he couldn't get enough of, wasn't it? This feeling of newness and hunger and longing. It had faded so quickly for us, and so he'd sought it elsewhere. And now I understood. I understood because I was behaving just as badly as he always had. I tried to shake off the uncomfortable thought.

"I was in the throes of insomnia last night," I told Finn. "Not very sexy."

I sat down at the table and he took the seat across from me.

"You should have called me," he said. "I'm sure I could have done something to help."

I put down the lid of the dish I'd just lifted. The scent of Hollandaise sauce wafted to my nose.

"What's your deal?" I asked sharply, suddenly in the mood for brutal honesty. "Come on. Let's be real here. I know a guy like you could have your pick. Why are you wasting all this time and energy on a married mother of two who'll be gone before the tide turns this afternoon?"

72

"You're leaving already?"

"Stay on topic, Finn. Answer me. When we joked around the other night, about you being a playboy who seduces lonely women, were we really circling the truth?"

He flashed his bad-boy grin at me again, but when I didn't budge, his expression changed. He glanced around as if the answer he needed to speak floated somewhere on the air above us.

"You guessed right," he said at last. "Sort of. This is what I do. I pick women who will only be in my life a short while. I show them a good time, and I have a good time myself. I keep it fresh and avoid entanglement. I'm not good at relationships, so it works for me."

"So it's a game for you," I said, wondering why the truth I'd expected to hear still sounded awful to my ears.

"Not a game," Finn said with emphasis. "Not at all. I don't believe in doing anything in life I don't feel wholeheartedly. But I also don't believe life is meant to be hard, and I figured out a while ago that most long-term relationships are work. Hard work. I just don't think that's how it's supposed to be."

"Maybe if you're with the right person, it's not hard work," I countered, trying to wrap my head around his philosophy.

Finn shrugged.

"Do you know anyone who has an easy marriage? You know, after a few years or a couple kids?"

Honestly, I didn't.

"No, not *easy*," I said. I thought of Tamara and Howard, Nate and Ian. "But good. I know some people who have excellent relationships. Maybe a little bit of work now and then, but I imagine they'd say the reward outweighs the sacrifice."

"I'm sure they would," Finn commented. "But isn't that what people do? Try to justify their choices?"

I started to object, but he interrupted me.

"I'm not saying there's anything wrong with it, if that's how people want to live. Let's face it: I'm in the minority, so there must be something about the whole 'til death do us part' deal that appeals to human nature. I'm just saying the long-term thing hasn't worked when I've tried it. Square peg, round hole - that sort of thing."

"Well, that I understand," I said honestly. I'd felt like a square peg trying to fit into a round hole for too many years now. It wasn't pleasant.

Finn reached across the table and lifted the lid from the dish in front of me.

"Let's eat before it gets cold," he said.

I tucked into my eggs Florentine because I couldn't think of anything more to say. I was still processing. Finn's candor had caught me a bit off guard. I'd expected him to continue the game, protest my characterization of him as a playboy, but instead he'd owned up to it and offered an explanation that made sense. I didn't agree with him, but I wasn't sure I could fault him.

"You said you're leaving?" he asked at last, breaking the silence that lingered between us as we ate.

I nodded.

"Why?"

"Why?" I parroted him. "Why? Because my girls' getaway isn't happening. Because Nana is dead. Because my marriage is over, my head is a mess, and I've got about five billion things to do."

The silence descended again. Not surprising, really, considering my tone had been about as friendly as the swift *swoosh* of a guillotine. Finn scraped egg yolk from his plate.

"So, your marriage is really over?" he asked. "Because of me? Because of...what happened?"

I dropped my fork in exasperation.

"No, not because of you." I exhaled, inhaled, pressed my fingers to the bridge of my nose. "Look, I told you. What happened with you was the first time I've ever - *ever* - done anything remotely...*bad*. But Skip? Bad is an art form for him. A way of being. And really, I'm not sure why I've put up with it for as long as I have. All I know is that when that valet handed me that lipstick, something inside me snapped."

Finn looked at me quizzically.

"The nanny's lipstick," I clarified. "Lola."

Finn's eyes widened, as if he was beginning to get the picture I'd so incompletely sketched for him. He laughed, then quickly tried to stifle it.

"What?" I demanded.

He shook his head, beginning to laugh in earnest.

"What?" I cried.

"It's just..." he began, putting a hand to his mouth and

trying to stifle his laughter. "Well…"

"What?" I insisted.

"Well, your husband's a serial philanderer, and you hired a nanny named Lola? Let me guess - young and hot? And you're surprised at this turn of events?"

I threw my napkin at him.

"Hey! This isn't funny!" I cried, but I could feel the laughter bubbling up inside me.

"No, it's not," he agreed, but he was still laughing.

"So stop laughing," I said, holding up my fork as if I would use it as a weapon.

Finn stood up, rounded the table, and took the fork from my hand. He placed it gently, tines down, on the edge of my plate. Something about this touch of decorum - his use of table manners when none were called for - threatened to unhinge me completely. He and I both stopped smiling as he raised me to stand, my hands held lightly in his.

"I have an idea," he said. "Stay. Stay just as you planned to, only with me instead of Tamara. I promise to give you as much space as you need. And I guarantee you I'll make it worth your while."

I shook my head, dropping my gaze from his eyes to my toes. He cupped my chin in his hand and raised my eyes to his.

"It's going to be rough when you head back to reality," he said sincerely. "A funeral, divorce, telling your kids. You know it won't be easy. Why hurry it? Have some fun first."

I looked away from him again, shaking free of his gentle grasp.

76

"Will I find a rather large surcharge for your services on my hotel bill?" I joked.

He pulled me to him, this time more firmly.

"I know you won't believe me," he said, an edge to his usually coy tone, "but prior to being defiled by you on the beach the other night it had been two years since I'd been, ah, *intimate* with anyone. I'm unorthodox, Eve, but I'm picky." He paused, then confessed, "I was there on the balcony when you pulled up in your little car. I saw you and I came back that night and I waited at the bar until you came in."

"That's kind of stalkerish," I said slowly.

"It is," he agreed. "Sorry. But you're beautiful. And I... Well, it had been two years."

He chuckled awkwardly, and I couldn't help but laugh, too. His charm was that persuasive. The compliments and the confession (not to mention the two-year thing - puh-*leeze*...) all seemed contrived to me, but I just couldn't help myself.

"Listen," I said. "You said something last night about going paddle boarding, maybe giving me a surfing lesson? I love to paddle board, and I've always wanted to learn to surf. So I'll stay for that. Nothing more."

"Deal," Finn agreed.

He'd given me his address but told me I wouldn't need it. He was right. Finn's place was just a three-minute walk from Ocean Manor. I paused at the end of the drive, feeling slightly queasy and wondering why. It hadn't exactly been a taxing workout getting here. Maybe guilt was finally getting to me? I pulled my phone from my bag and checked. No response from Skip. No texts from the boys. Sadness tugged at me. I dropped my phone back into my bag and tried to shake it off.

I entered the code Finn had given me into the keypad by the gates, then watched as they swung open. My house in Jamestown had gates and an imposing driveway, too, but somehow I felt small here. I wore my swimsuit and a beach cover-up and flip-flops, and I toted sunscreen and towels and a rash guard in an L.L. Bean bag. I felt underdressed even in comparison to the precisely-manicured shrubbery along the driveway. Then I rounded the bend and saw the house.

How to describe it? It was the most amazing fusion of modern architecture and old New England feel I have ever seen. It was flat-roofed and cedar-shingled, with cantilevers jutting out here and there, framed by the open water beyond, as if the living space was suspended over the Atlantic. It was stunning. Finn lived here, and he was an architect by trade, so I assumed the design was his, and I wasn't quite sure what to do with that. His ruggedly attractive good looks had, to be honest, left me looking down on him just a smidge. I'd automatically tucked him away in my pretty-boy file, and I realized that may have been unfair. No. Strike "may have."

Except…

"Hey babe," he said, opening the front door before I'd fully reached it.

Hey babe?

Who said that?

Outside of Cranston, anyway?

"Hey," I replied.

I turned my cheek to his kiss as I entered the foyer.

"Kidding," he said earnestly. "The 'babe' thing. That was a joke. Clearly my tone didn't carry."

I laughed lightly, as if I'd known all along. And then I took in the view.

The entire rear of the house was glass, and the view was of the Atlantic below, the blue sky above, and the thin line of the horizon between. My own house in Jamestown had an impressive water view, but this was a whole new level. This was like being on a houseboat. A massive, architecturally-stunning houseboat.

"Wow," I sighed. "Nice back yard."

"Not too shabby, eh?" Finn agreed.

"Well, hello," I said, crouching to pet the giant Maine coon cat who was suddenly circling my legs, rubbing solidly against me. "Oscar Wilde, I presume? Don't be shy," I joked.

"Hmm," Finn said. "He usually doesn't like women. But then, who wouldn't want to wrap himself around your legs?"

I rolled my eyes.

"I believe we agreed I am here for water sports. None of your hanky-panky," I said with a smirk.

Finn laughed.

"All right. Come here. Check this out."

He grabbed my hand and bounded toward the glass doors at the far end of the living room. I laughed, sailing along behind him, trying to take in my surroundings. The decor was homier than I might have imagined. None of that sterile bachelor pad feel. There were deep sofas and lush Persian carpets, eclectic art and books everywhere. I wondered if this was the work of a decorator or a true expression of Finn's self.

"Well?" he asked.

He had opened the doors and led me out onto the teak deck. He pulled a small remote control from a dock mounted just outside the door. He pressed a button and the floor beneath us hummed.

"I never had quite the right place to store my boards," he said by way of explanation.

I watched as a massive drawer slid out from beneath the deck. Right under our feet was storage for no fewer than six surf and paddle boards. Each lay nestled in a cradle designed for it perfectly.

"Wow," I said, awestruck. "You made this?"

Finn nodded.

"With a little help from a friend whose business is retractable awnings. I took his mechanics and adapted them, then built this storage unit with custom space for each board. How perfect is that?"

"Perfect," I affirmed.

"Want to start with a paddle?" he asked, tipping his head toward the calm seas at the edge of his property. "There's not much surf now, but it's supposed to pick up later."

"Sounds great," I said.

Finn slid two boards from their spaces, and I noticed that there were paddles stored neatly in beside them. Finn passed me the paddles, then hefted the boards under his arms and started walking toward the water.

"Hey," I protested. "I can carry my own board."

Finn laughed.

"Of course you can. That's what makes this such a lovely gesture on my part." He paused as he reached the beach. "I was raised a gentleman."

"You were?" I teased. "And what happened to you after that?"

He dropped the boards into the sand and reached out to grab my rear end playfully. I cried out in mock indignation.

"Careful," I cautioned, smiling devilishly. "I've got not one paddle, but two."

"Promises, promises," Finn intoned.

I dropped one paddle and brought the other around ever-so-lightly into contact with that delightfully-taut ass of his. Even in baggy board shorts there was no mistaking the build underneath.

"Hey," Finn cried.

He took hold of the paddle and used it to reel me in. In short order, the paddle had been tossed aside, and his lips were on mine.

I had the thought: *I am too damn old for this.*

Then the countering thought, in Tamara's voice and

sassy tone: *Shut up and enjoy, bitch.*

The truth was that my mind was a mess, but something inside me simply kept moving toward what felt best, and what felt best in the moment was Finn. My body pressed against his. The soft curve of my breast against the firm cut of his chest. The swell of my hip against the wall of his abs. And then this: my head falling back, my hair spilling between my shoulder blades, tickling, while his hand ran lightly over my throat, brushed my ear, cupped the back of my head. I felt his lips, first at my breastbone, then moving softly upward, caressing the ridges of my throat while I swallowed instinctively. Then his tongue was at my earlobe, lightly brushing the tip so sensually I felt it everywhere. His hand at the nape of my neck sent sparks flying. Nerve endings on fire, I drew his bottom lip in between my teeth, nipped at it gently.

"Oh, god."

The paddle boards lay side-by-side in the sand, and I found myself reclining on one. The grooved rubber surface, meant for balance and ease on the feet during a long paddle, chafed at my back as Finn leaned in to me.

"Eve," Finn breathed, my name melting on his tongue.

I melted.

Chemistry. That was the only word for it. Or maybe *want. Need.* There was something between me and Finn that I could not otherwise describe. My body responded to his in ways I had only ever imagined before. Every time he touched me, I felt a longing that had been dormant for only too long. He made me feel like a stranger to myself, and I loved it.

82

The cry of a seagull overhead brought me back to reality. I realized we were on a beach in full daylight, making out like a couple of teenagers. I wriggled out from under him and stood.

Again, there was a flash of nausea, this time insistent enough that I worried I might be coming down with something. How else could I go from passion to nausea in a nanosecond? But it passed, and I wondered again if it was just my conscience kicking in.

"You're a tease, you know that?" Finn said, standing and whispering in my ear.

"We're on a beach in broad daylight. You really have to stop enticing me to behave so badly."

"It's a private beach. My beach," Finn reasoned. "And my new neighbor has so much goddamned security, I doubt anyone could get into this area unless they belong here."

"Yeah," I said curiously. "I noticed all the Secret Service-looking guys on the walk up. Who's your neighbor? A former President or something?"

"Pop star. Taylor Something."

"Oh."

I didn't know much about pop culture, and I couldn't recall the last name, but I knew who Finn was talking about. The pretty blonde girl with all the venomous songs about exes. Max had quite a crush on her, and I'd heard she'd bought a place in Rhode Island.

"You better watch out," I teased Finn. "Tick her off and she'll write a song about you."

83

"Ah, no worries there. She's not my type."

"Really? Blonde, half your age, and super-rich doesn't do it for you?"

Finn stepped in and put his hands on my hips.

"'Fraid not. I prefer red hair, dangerous curves, and aged to perfection."

I punched his arm and let out a laugh.

"You are such a *player*! Good god, what a line!"

"You just don't know how to take a compliment."

I shook my head, still laughing, then pulled off my beach coverup and grabbed a board and paddle.

"Come on," I said, aiming the board into the water. "Try to keep up."

As I bent to fasten the leash around my ankle, I noticed we had company. Oscar Wilde had made his way down to the beach and was mewing loudly at Finn.

"Sorry, buddy, she's my date today. You stay on land."

"I don't believe you really take that cat out paddleboarding," I said as I stood on my board, getting my balance and starting to skim across the light chop of the surface.

Finn gave me a look.

"Okay, buddy," he said to the cat. "You're in." To me he said, "Be right back."

Finn sprinted from the beach to the house while I paddled in lazy circles over the water. He returned with a tiny, fluorescent yellow life preserver. I shook my head in disbelief as he put it on the cat. As soon as Finn slid his board into the water, Oscar Wilde leapt on. He stood at the nose of the board, his tail swishing contentedly, as Finn paddled over. It was the strangest thing I'd ever seen. And funny as hell.

"Well?" Finn asked.

"I stand corrected," I chuckled.

"Hey," he said, his tone turning serious. "Are you feeling okay?"

Truthfully, I wasn't. I felt slightly dizzy, and the queasiness I'd felt earlier had returned.

"I think I just need to get moving," I said.

We paddled along, but even though the sight of Oscar Wilde on the nose of the board could have amused me forever, I realized before long that I definitely wasn't well.

"Hey Finn," I said, "I think I need to go back."

Please, dear God, let me not puke in front of this guy.

We paddled back to the beach. I stepped off the board and immediately sat down in the sand.

"Jesus, Eve," Finn said. "You're white as a sheet."

I tried keeping it light.

"We redheads don't tan. Our freckles just merge."

"Seriously," he said, kneeling before me and unfastening the leash from my ankle. "You look like - "

And that's when I lost it. With this gorgeous guy mere inches away, I turned and vomited into the sand.

Finn stood, and I imagined him fleeing. Instead, he returned with a beach towel and wiped at the edges of my mouth. Then, before I could register what he was doing enough to protest, he scooped me up into his arms and began carrying me toward the house.

85

"Finn," I began in protest. "I'm fine. I just..."

"Eve, clearly you are not fine. Were you drinking last night?"

"No."

"And did this just hit you suddenly?"

I shook my head.

"I'm sorry," I said. "I almost called to cancel. I didn't feel terribly sick, but I didn't feel well, either. A little dizzy, and just...not quite right."

Finn settled me onto a lounge chair on the deck. He disappeared into the house for a moment, then returned with a blanket and a glass of water. I noticed then that I was shivering in spite of the warm day.

"Here," Finn said, tucking the blanket around me and handing me the glass of water. "Small sips."

"Thank you, Florence Nightingale," I smiled.

Just then, a patch of fluorescent yellow bobbing across the lawn caught my attention.

"Oh, poor Oscar Wilde!" I laughed. "He's still got his life vest on!"

The cat trotted up onto the deck and stood at Finn's feet, looking up at him with an expression that indicated he didn't care for being left behind, and wearing a life jacket to boot. Finn freed the cat from the little vest, and he darted into the house.

"Feeling any better?" Finn asked, sitting on the edge of my chaise.

"A bit," I said.

"You're still awfully pale."

"I'm still a redhead."

"Well, you're an even whiter shade of pale than usual, then."

"I think I just need to get back to the hotel and lie down," I said. "I'm so sorry. Way to take our afternoon from fun to gross, eh?"

Finn shrugged.

"You are not at your hottest when you're puking," he admitted.

He gathered up my things, and I put my beach coverup back on. He insisted on driving me the extremely short distance back to the hotel and then walking me to my suite.

"Thank you," I said sincerely.

"Get some rest," he said. "I'll check in on you later."

I peeled off my swimsuit and pulled on my nightshirt, then took the waste bin from the bathroom and set it by the side of the bed – just in case. At that point I felt more dizzy than nauseous.

I checked my phone once more. Still no return call from Skip. Max had texted with a request for a variety of expensive new lacrosse gear. No word from Eli. I turned the ringer down and crawled into bed. I pulled up the covers against the shivers that shook me, and after some time, I fell deeply asleep.

I woke soaked in sweat, with Finn leaning over me.

"Wake up, Eve," he said urgently.

It took me a minute to orient myself. I was still in bed at Ocean Manor, sweating and shivering simultaneously. The windows were black with night. Caleb hovered in the doorway, and Finn thrust something in front of me.

"Did you take these?" he asked.

It registered then. My prescription meds. He was holding all the bottles in his hands. I vaguely remembered sweeping them into the trash, and I wondered how he'd gotten them. Perhaps housekeeping had pulled them from the bin.

"Are you supposed to take all of these?" Finn asked.

I nodded.

"Did you take more than you should?"

"No," I said. "I didn't take them at all."

"You forgot?"

I shook my head.

"No. I didn't want to take them anymore. So I stopped."

"Caleb, call for an ambulance," Finn barked. "This is withdrawal."

"No," I cried. "No ambulance."

Caleb hesitated.

"Caleb, call," Finn said, his voice low, and the boy went to the phone. "Those are some serious drugs, Eve. You can't just stop taking them. You'll have a heart attack, for chrissakes. Why on earth did you do that?"

"It seemed decisive," I said meekly.

Finn laughed in spite of himself.

"Well, come on," he said.

He dressed me like a rag doll, replacing my nightshirt with yoga pants, a tee shirt, and a cardigan as I limply complied. At just about any other time, I would have found a scene like this to be unfathomably embarrassing, but at the moment, I felt too awful to care. As Finn slid my feet into ballet shoes, Caleb's head appeared in the doorway.

"They're on their way," he said.

From there it was a blur, my mind taking in fragments of the events as they unfolded. I was shaking and dizzy as they carried me out on a stretcher, but still alert enough to register horror at being removed from Ocean Manor by ambulance, and then relief that it seemed to be so late at night only the staff witnessed my exit. I noticed, even, that the EMTs worked quickly and quietly, as if the salty old-money feel of the grand hotel inspired decorum in any situation.

The brightly-lit ambulance, however, made my heart race. I'd only ever seen one person loaded into an ambulance – my father when I was seventeen – and he hadn't returned. I saw Finn's face for a moment, and his lips were moving, but I couldn't make out what he said. Then he was gone, and I felt a panic attack closing in on me. I tried to say so, but someone simply said, "Shhh" and put an oxygen mask over my face. I felt overwhelmingly sleepy then, as if I had been the one exerting the effort of carrying me from my suite to the ambulance, so that now simply keeping my eyes open was an effort. I noticed an I.V. bag over my head, though I hadn't felt a needle enter my arm. I felt warm. The shivering stopped.

The next thing I registered was being carried into the

89

hospital. I was moved from the stretcher onto a gurney, all of which happened as if in a dream. Then I lay, for minutes or for hours, in what appeared to be a busy corridor, drifting in and out of sleep as men and women in scrubs bustled by. "We're admitting you," a female voice said at last, and I was moved again. This time, though, I felt more alert. When we reached the room, I was able to move on wobbly legs from the gurney to the bed.

A woman who smelled of cigarettes tucked me in and arranged various lines and wires about me.

"I'm Candy," she said. "Press this button if you need me."

I fell back to sleep before I could nod.

And for some reason, I dreamed of Skip.

Chapter **Five**

I met Skip almost exactly six months before my mother would die, though of course I didn't know that at the time. All I knew then was that the very good looking, well-dressed and slightly-older-than-me associate teaching my real estate law class was flirting with me.

And I liked it.

Of course, what wasn't to like? It was a real estate law class. Aside from the exciting prospect of adverse possession, what was there? Endless discussion of tenancies? Lectures on the finer points of probate and inheritance tax law? If not for Skip, I may not have remained conscious through any of it.

That he was an incurable flirt was obvious from the start. He had just about every female student eating from the palm of his hand within the first five minutes of the very first class. The thing was, while he was good-looking, he wasn't *that* good-looking. What did it, though – what made him irresistible – was his personality. He was funny, and he knew it. He liked having an audience, and he played it up. I had the sense that he could listen to himself talk all day. His cockiness should have been off-putting, but he knew how to balance it with just enough self-deprecating humor that he came across as charming.

On the last day of class, as I made my way out of the building and across the lawn, thinking I'd probably never see him again, Skip was suddenly close behind me. His lips almost grazed my ear as he spoke.

"So, now that we no longer have that whole student-teacher issue to worry about, when are we going out?"

My heart leapt. And then I was pretty sure I felt his hand swipe lightly across my backside. Did men do that anymore? I mean, this was 1996, after all. The modern age. And yet...

I stopped walking and turned to face him. He must have pulled his tie off as soon as class had ended; the collar of his Oxford shirt was endearingly askew. His fair hair curled haphazardly about his face, as if he'd just run a hand through it. And for the first time I noticed his eyes. In the sunlight, they weren't the hazel I'd assumed, but a deep, mesmerizing blue. I realized I was staring, and I dropped my gaze.

"Cat got your tongue?" Skip inquired, tipping my chin up with his forefingers. "A date, Miss Martin. I'm asking you out on a date."

Though the age difference between us was slight, I felt like a child gazing up at him. He regarded me as if I were amusing to him in a way only he understood, and the effect was unsettling.

"Is that what that was?" I asked, trying to summon the flirting skills that came to me so easily with other men. "I wasn't sure."

"I will be more specific, then," he said, the corner of his mouth still twitching as if on the verge of a smile. "Dinner. Tonight. I'll pick you up at seven."

I very nearly agreed. Skip had this way about him that made agreement the natural option. But, for reasons I couldn't have identified in that moment, he also made me slightly uncomfortable.

"Sorry," I said. "I have plans tonight."

The smile vanished from the corner of his lips. He looked confused.

"Tomorrow night, then?" he asked, a little less certain.

I hesitated. What was it about him that both compelled me and made me uneasy all at once? I'd been out with a half-dozen guys since the start of law school, and I usually felt like I had the upper hand.

"Okay," I said. "But make it six-thirty. I have to be up early the next morning. Here, let me give you my address."

I opened a notebook, but Skip shook his head.

"I know where you live," he said slyly.

"That's kind of creepy," I said.

Skip laughed.

"It was on the class list," he said. "Until about five minutes ago, I was your professor, remember?"

I blushed furiously, feeling foolish. Why hadn't I thought of that? The amused look had returned to Skip's face.

"Of course," I said. "I'll see you tomorrow night."

And then I took off before I could say another stupid thing.

Our first date fell on one of those perfect days that happen now and then in Boston in the late spring, when Mother Nature decides we should have a preview of summer and a reminder of all that is wonderful about the city. I had the windows of my tiny apartment open, the curtains blowing against the wrought-iron grating as I tried to decide what to wear. I settled on a simple sleeveless black dress and flats. I put my hair up and then let it down again. I arranged it around my shoulders, and I chose a pair of silver teardrop earrings. I looked in the mirror and decided this would do. I'd fit in if we went someplace nice, but I wouldn't look overdressed if we ended up in a bar.

I suspected Skip came from money – he had that easy, expensive look about him that my experiences as a scholarship student at Mount Holyoke and Harvard had taught me came from never having to worry about paying the rent. My suspicions were confirmed when he arrived for our date with a car and driver.

"It's such a beautiful night," I said, a little bit disappointed. "We could walk to dinner."

"It has a sunroof," he said as he led me to the car.

The driver held the rear door open and Skip and I slid inside.

"There's this great little place in the North End," Skip explained, pressing a button. The roof opened above us, and the last rays of daylight filtered in through the yellow-green tree branches above. A light breeze stirred as the car pulled away from the curb. "A little far to walk."

"Oh," I said, taking in my surroundings.

There was a television set and a phone in the car. I thought briefly of my parents and what they would think of that. My mother still worked two jobs, and my father had, too, until his death of a heart attack at age forty-one. Their house still had only one phone, mounted on the wall in the kitchen. My mother's car was nearly twenty years old. She would never have one of these mobile phones that seemed to be growing in popularity.

"You look lovely," Skip said, bringing me back.

He leaned in and his hand closed over mine. He kissed my cheek, and he lingered long enough that I could smell his cologne, faint and sexy. I closed my eyes, feeling a light rush from his proximity, and then I felt him lean away.

I opened my eyes to find him watching me, that same bemused look on his face. I looked away and he laughed. I had the sense we were playing some version of the game 'chicken.'

"Come on," he said. "Tell me about you. Did my class inspire you to make real estate law your focus?"

I chuckled and shook my head.

"Sorry, you did a great job with the material, but…"

"What?" he teased. "I didn't leave you with a hankering for a good boundary line dispute?" He rolled his eyes "Seriously? I'm only going on my second year at Cavanaugh & Stein, and if I have to look at another title abstract, I'll stick a pen in my eye. I have no idea how people do that for a living."

"So what do you want to do?" I asked.

"White collar litigation. Guys caught with their hands in the company cookie jar, that sort of thing."

"Why?" I asked.

Skip shrugged.

"Why not?" He rubbed his thumb and forefinger together. "Good money."

"Is there any such thing as bad money?" I mused, and Skip laughed.

"I don't suppose there is," he said.

The restaurant Skip had chosen was first-date perfection. It was a tiny place, elegantly appointed, all candlelight and white linen. Skip ordered a bottle of wine with a name I couldn't pronounce. He proposed a toast.

"Here's to leaving real estate law behind us and exploring much, much more interesting topics," he said.

I was pretty sure he was undressing me with his eyes. I blushed as I raised my glass.

My dinner was the most amazing shrimp scampi I'd ever tasted, the linguine fresh and al dente. Skip had veal, and poked fun at me when I told him I didn't eat land animals. He claimed eating seafood was much more detrimental to the environment than factory farming, and he made his argument so deftly and with such casual humor, I could see he'd be deadly in a court room.

"Excellent argument, Counsellor," I said, working to keep a smile on my face. "But veal is cruel and vulgar, and I hope you've brought a tooth brush if you intend to kiss me good night with that mouth."

Skip looked stunned, and then thrilled. Years later I would understand that this was but one example of what it was that made me the lucky girl who finally enticed Skip Wolcott to tie the knot. I challenged him. Ironically, once we were married, I became just as pliant as all the other girls he'd dated, and he lost interest. But neither of us knew that first night just how marriage to Skip would wear me down.

After dinner, we walked a short distance and found a café where we had gelato.

"Will this cleanse my palate sufficiently for a kiss?" Skip asked, waving his spoon at me.

"Maybe," I grinned. "If it can take care of the garlic from my meal, then you might be all right."

"I didn't want to question your menu choice," Skip teased, "but…"

I stuck my tongue out at him.

The driver circled the city before taking me home. I learned that Skip had lived here when he was younger, when his father had been at the height of his career as a surgeon. They'd spent summers in Newport, and Skip had boarded at Morefield Academy from age ten on, but he had so many memories of Boston, it seemed there wasn't a place we passed that lacked a story. I listened, watching the stars through the open sunroof.

At my door, Skip leaned in for a kiss, pressing heavily against me. I yielded, but only so far.

"That was a nice evening," Skip said. "Aren't you going to invite me in?"

"That *was* a nice evening," I agreed, "but like I said when we made the date, I have an early day tomorrow."

"Really? What's all that important now that classes are over?"

"My internship," I replied. "I need to be downtown by 8 a.m."

Skip left with a hasty, disappointed kiss.

It was only when I was in bed and turning out the light that I realized: while I now knew Skip's entire life story, he knew almost nothing about me. The one time he'd asked, he'd talked over my reply.

The truth was, the more I got to know Skip, the less I liked him. He was self-centered and arrogant. When he did things for me, it was with the clear expectation of gratitude on my part. And yet I kept

97

dating him. I found him appealing in a way that left me wondering if I was a masochist. I felt shy and uncertain in his presence, breathless and yearning when he left.

On the morning of our fifth date, I arrived to find a dozen red roses waiting for me on my desk at work. It was embarrassing. There I was, an intern in a tiny cubicle at the major law firm where I'd worked for only two weeks, and my entire desk was overshadowed by this formal arrangement of flowers I'd never have chosen for myself. I liked peonies, hydrangea, lilies, even wildflowers. But roses? Red roses?

I read the card:

Can't wait to see you tonight.

xxx,

Skip

I got the implicit message. Fifth date. A fair amount of pawing and making out on the previous three. This was it. The Big Night.

"Should I sleep with him?" I asked Tamara over the phone as I shaved my legs in preparation for the date.

"Fuck, yeah," she said. "I mean, how long has it been since you got laid?"

I thought of my last relationship, with Wes and his sweaty hands and the horrible noises he made during sex. Mentally, I counted back to our last damp, grunting roll in the hay.

"Six months? Maybe seven?"

"Yeah, go for it."

"But he's kind of a jerk," I said.

"Well, you're not gonna *marry* him," Tamara sighed. "He's hot, right?"

"Very much so," I said, thinking of the way my stomach had turned to Jell-O while we'd been kissing and groping on my sofa three nights earlier.

"So fuck him," Tamara said. "But just do it like a man does. With no attachments or expectations. No hearts and roses, none of that shit."

"He's big into roses," I said.

"Well, just don't fall for it," Tamara cautioned.

I thought of her words later, as Skip and I lay in my bed, blissfully exhausted. I wondered if humans were just not as sophisticated as we'd like to think we are, if we were all just slaves to chemistry. Four hours earlier, I'd been telling Tamara Skip was "kind of a jerk," and now, one good, solid, headboard-banging lay later, I was grinning stupidly, my head against his chest as he whispered sweet, predictable things in my ear.

I drifted off to sleep determined to get my head on straight in the morning. I couldn't let this happen again.

Two months later, Skip and I were still dating. Well, if you wanted to call it that. Most of our time together was spent in bed. I took this as a good sign. It meant I was heeding Tamara's advice, keeping it from evolving into a "real" relationship. The funny thing was, Skip kept trying to make it something more.

When he heard that Tamara and her brother Nate would be in town for the weekend, he insisted on taking us all out sightseeing. We went on a whirlwind tour of the Freedom Trail (by chauffeured car, of course), then hit a Rex Sox game, and by evening wound up at a party on a yacht in the harbor – some massive thing owned by a friend of Skip's parents.

"Holy crap," Tamara said, when she and Nate and I finally had a moment without Skip. "What have you done to that man?"

"What?" I asked.

"What?" Nate mocked. "Oh please, little-miss-doe-eyed-innocence. Give it a rest."

"You were supposed to just fuck him, like a guy, no strings attached," Tamara reminded me accusingly. "Now he's whisking us all over frigging Boston in an effort to impress us so he can thereby impress *you*. Not good."

I grabbed a cracker topped with salmon pate from a tray as a waiter passed. I glanced over at the bar, where Skip was engaged in conversation with an older couple. He was wearing a pink Oxford shirt, the collar popped over his navy blazer. Tamara caught me gazing at him appreciatively and gave me a stern look.

"Hey. What did we learn from *Pretty in Pink*?" she asked sharply.

"That subtlety wasn't John Hughes' strong suit?" Nate offered, swirling his gin and tonic before taking a sip. Even in his twenties, Nate was an elegant drinker.

I laughed. Tamara pretended she hadn't heard either of us.

"That blonde guys in pink shirts with popped collars are bad news," she said succinctly. "Especially if they're rich and have bedroom eyes."

"Bedroom eyes," I sighed, glad Tamara had furnished

the term that escaped me every time I took in Skip's heavy-lidded baby blues. I looked back over at him. He had finished his conversation with the older couple and was now batting his eyelashes at the pretty young bartender as he gathered up a fresh round of drinks. "Yes, that's what you'd call them."

"You are in for a world of hurt with that one, sister," Tamara said.

If only I had a nickel for the times I'd thought back on her words over the years.

I meant to end things with Skip, but two things happened: first his father died, then my mother.

I met Skip's father only once, and under the worst of circumstances. He'd been diagnosed with colon cancer, discovered late, and was given a matter of weeks to live. The irony of this happening to a famed surgeon was lost on no one. Skip plucked me from work without warning, and in the car on the way to Newport he'd told me his father was dying. We rode in silence the rest of the way, his hand gripping mine as if hanging on for dear life.

Arriving at the Wolcott residence in Newport amidst a family crisis was baptism by fire. Though I knew Skip came from money, nothing could have prepared me for the Ocean Road mansion, the staff in uniform, the family members attired so neatly I felt shabby in my favorite Gap skirt, blouse and scuffed patent-leather flats.

I learned that Skip was ten years younger than the next-youngest of his four older brothers. "I was a pleasant surprise," he said, stiffly introducing me to a line of suit-clad men who appeared to me as Skip's future personified. They all looked the same: the blonde curls in varying degrees of recession, the features just strong enough to be masculine, yet soft enough to suggest wealth and leisure. Looking from one to the next was like perusing time-lapse photography. Their wives hung on their arms like accessories, beautiful and silent.

And then I met Kitty.

She entered the room slowly, teetering on her high heels as if the burden of her husband's illness was weighing on her physically, yet once my eyes rose to her face I could see she was in full control of the situation at hand. Her makeup was flawless, though the moles were startling. She wore black, already in mourning, but a poppy-colored pin affixed to her breast caught my eye. As I moved in, I could see it was in the shape of a serpent. Her sons peeled themselves away from their wives and fluttered about their mother, fawning.

"Mother, this is Eve," Skip said, pulling me near. "I've told you about her?"

I held out my hand and Kitty ignored it.

"Of course," she said, running her eyes over me, head to toe. A look of doubt crossed her face. "The ingénue at Boston ballet?"

"Ah, no, Mother," Skip said haltingly.

"Oh my," Kitty said, a hand drifting to her chest as if she were embarrassed by her mistake. "Surely not the new face of that cosmetics company?"

"Mother," Skip said, his voice a note lower. "Eve is the law student I was telling you about. One more year and she'll pass the bar."

"Of *course*," Kitty breathed. "And law is such a fascinating profession for young women now. So utterly devoid of femininity, yet thanks to Gloria Steinem and her ilk, that's no worry for some girls any more, is it?"

I tried to get past her use of the word 'ilk.' I noticed she delivered a piercing glance at one of her daughters-in-law, a forty-ish woman in a business suit, her hair pulled into a tight bun.

"Jenny can tell you all about making a law career your life, Ava," Kitty sneered, her gaze still directed at that one cowering daughter-in-law. "Why, if you can't have children, it's a very good option."

"Eve," Skip corrected his mother. "Her name is Eve."

I watched as Jenny fled the room. Her husband didn't budge.

I decided then and there not to marry Skip, not to have one more date with him, not even one more knee-weakening roll in the hay. His was clearly a family that couldn't keep the "fun" in dysfunctional.

Kitty moved past us and settled onto a sofa in the next room. One of her sons scurried to bring her a drink.

"Your father is expecting you," she called over her

shoulder to Skip.

I followed Skip up the main staircase with a sense of dread. I didn't want to meet Dr. Wolcott, the man who had chosen that woman for his wife. I didn't want to spend another second in the cold of that house in Newport. I wanted desperately to close my eyes and click my heels and find myself back in my tiny apartment in Boston.

I shouldn't have worried.

Even gravely ill and confined to bed, Dr. Wolcott was a warm, welcoming presence. Skip went to him without hesitation, wrapping him in a hug that seemed hesitant only out of concern for his father's fragile condition. He sat on the edge of the bed and I took a chair across the room. I felt like an intruder at first, observing the easy rapport between father and son, but Dr. Wolcott quickly drew me into the conversation. He told me stories about Skip as a child: learning to swim in the light surf at Easton's Beach and emerging with jellyfish in his swim trunks, "borrowing" a boat as a teenager and nearly outrunning the Harbor Master.

He asked me about my family, and I told him about our summer vacations in Misquamicut, always in a rental that smelled slightly of low tide, and how my father and I would spend a fair portion of every day at the beach building a massive wall and moat around the beach blanket where my mother lounged. I had a moment of sudden self-consciousness, realizing I was sharing mundane details with a man who'd spent his career pulling people back from the brink of death, and who now lay, literally, on his own death bed. But Dr. Wolcott smiled

104

at me, and Skip smiled at me, and I realized I couldn't make good on my earlier resolve. I couldn't banish Skip from my life.

The late-night drive back to Boston from Newport passed, as before, without a word, and with Skip and I stiffly hand-in-hand. But something had shifted. With the driver silhouetted before us and lights passing on either side, we sat. Miles Davis played lightly over the car speakers, and when we arrived at my apartment, Skip followed me inside as lightly as if moving on cat's feet. We undressed and climbed into bed, curling around one another without passion or pretense. We slept and woke entangled together.

Dr. Wolcott passed away four days later, a quiet death discovered by the Hospice nurse in the early morning. Skip got the call as he was dressing for work, and he headed to my office instead of to his own. He waited at the door for me to arrive. When I saw him, in suit pants and shirt but without a tie or jacket, bereft instead of cocky, I knew. I went into my office just long enough to tell them that, for the second time that week, I would need a personal day.

I'd barely turned my key in the lock and pressed my door open when Skip crumbled. I folded him into my arms and half-carried him to the sofa as he sobbed. The heft of his weight against me, so deeply burdened by grief, was startling. It reminded me of my own father's death when I was seventeen, a most unwelcome recollection. But this was familiar territory: the lurching, unstoppable pain of death. The knowledge that your world has been altered irrevocably. The realization that it happens to everyone, and yet you don't care. You just don't want it to happen to you. Not now, not ever. God, I knew this, and I felt Skip's pain at my very core.

I cradled him in my arms, still not fully able to believe that this grieving soul was the same superficial man I thought I knew, and my heart began to open. I might love him, I thought. I could. Maybe I already did.

Dr. Wolcott was laid to rest in Swan Point Cemetery three days later, in a small family ceremony to which I was not invited, as I was not family. Skip stayed at his brother's house in Providence that night, where his family had gathered to mourn, and when I came home from work the next day, I found him sitting on my doorstep.

"Hey," I said gently, putting my hand on his shoulder.

But when he looked up at me, I saw that the old Skip had returned. He grinned devilishly and swatted my rear as he stood.

"Go on," he said, nodding at me door. "Get that ass of yours into something hot and short, and let's go get drinks."

I did as I was told.

And so it went. Skip behaved as though his father's death hadn't happened, but for me, something had changed. I imagined Skip's childhood, raised by that horrible ice woman, too much younger than his brothers to count on them for support, and shuttled off to boarding school and summer camps at an age so tender it broke my heart. I saw clearly the genuine love he'd shared with his father, as well as Skip's desire to impress him, but for someone as busy as Dr. Wolcott, time with his children was surely a rare thing. A man didn't end up with his name on a wing of a hospital because he'd been at hockey games or playing catch in the back yard. The notion of Skip as a child gave me a clearer picture of how the puzzle pieces had fit together to create the man who sent ostentatious flowers and had us chauffeured around a delightfully walk-able city. It softened me to him, and yes, before long, it had happened. I looked at him one morning, absentmindedly tying his tie in the doorway of my bathroom, and I realized I loved him.

In hindsight, that seems so foolish. So stupid. The classic mistake of the gullible girl who thinks only she understands the wounded soul of the bad boy and can change him. But of course, I wasn't thinking of it in such terms at the time. I just knew that I loved him, that love wasn't logical, and now I was along for the ride.

We spent Thanksgiving that year with his family, an experience that only affirmed I'd fallen for Skip, and hard. Any sane person would have chosen a root canal over more time with that clan. Skip's brothers were a boisterous clutch of look-alikes I couldn't tell apart. In the morning they played rugby, and came back sweaty and filthy and still somehow looking like money personified. By cocktail hour they'd changed into khakis, crisp shirts and navy blazers. I had trouble picking Skip out of the group; it was like trying to find your own yellow lab in a pack of the same.

I learned that Jenny, the daughter-in-law Kitty had skewered in my presence on my previous visit, had filed for divorce. She, her rigid style, and her uncooperative ovaries were the subject of countless jokes over dinner. I was chilled by the delight with which this family bashed a person who'd been one of their own until just recently. I made a mental note never to cross the Wolcotts.

The day after Thanksgiving, Skip and I crossed the bridge and headed north to Warwick to visit my mother. Halfway there I balked, offering once again that I could go alone. The thought of pulling up in front of the tiny ranch house I'd grown up in, especially having come straight from the Wolcott's elegant Newport mansion, became more unbearable the closer we drew.

Skip said nothing as we made our way up the path to the front door. I noticed that the house looked smaller, even, than I remembered it, and the vinyl siding was stained with mold. The yard was in desperate need of trimming, and the flower beds were overrun with weeds. I thought of the money I sent my mother regularly, parsed from the life insurance policy my father had left to me because he knew how poorly his wife would manage a lump sum. I wondered if she'd developed bad habits beyond the cigarettes and lottery tickets.

It was worse than I could have guessed. We entered the house and found my mother propped in her recliner, a mask over her mouth and nose and tubes trailing to a tank at her side. Though she'd always been thin, now she was gaunt. Her eyes were sunken, her skin jaundiced. It had been too long since I'd visited – three, maybe four months – but still it seemed impossible that such a drastic transformation had occurred in that span of time.

"Skip, give us a moment," I said, and he gladly retreated to the car.

"Lung cancer," she said wryly when we were alone. "Of course. All those times you hid my cigarettes. You were right once again."

I didn't want to be right.

"Why didn't you tell me?"

"What were you going to do? Quit law school and take care of me? After all those years your father and I worked to see that you'd have it better?" Her breath rattled in her chest. "I've got good insurance," she said. "That's one thing that came of working. They send someone in to check on me, and when it gets bad enough, they'll send Hospice."

I teared up. My mother and I were not close – she always seemed to regard me as alien, as if there'd been a mixup at the hospital on the day I was born – but she was the only family I had left. I was the only child of two only children. Was there anything lonelier in the world?

She wouldn't talk more about her condition, and she wouldn't hear of me coming to stay with her. She tapped the remote control on the arm of her chair and raised the volume of the television.

"You seen this one?" she asked, waving the remote at a show I didn't recognize.

I shook my head. We sat without saying anything for another few minutes, and I wondered if she was really watching the show or just sitting and staring like I was. I stood, thinking maybe I should leave.

"That boyfriend of yours coming back in, or did I scare him off?" my mother said without looking away from the TV. "I've got pot pies if you want to stay for dinner."

So Skip came back in, and we heated pot pies in my mother's kitchen with the pea green appliances circa 1970-something. I took him down the hall and showed him the room that had been mine, still decorated in purple and pink, with unicorn stickers affixed to one wall and a 10,000 Maniacs poster pinned to the closet door. A sewing machine sat on my desk now, and boxes of fabric were piled on the bed. I tried to remember if I knew that my mother had taken up sewing.

We ate dinner on our laps in front of the television, me pushing the chicken aside and eating the vegetables out of the pot pie. Skip looked notably out of place, like a crown prince paying a visit to a tenement, yet somehow he gave no indication of the distress I was sure he must be feeling. He chatted my mother up and made her laugh as easily as he did any female. She giggled and talked with him in a way that verged on flirtatious. I cleared our trays in disbelief as she and Skip found common ground discussing some talk show where people hit their relatives with folding chairs. It was only as I reached the kitchen that I realized my mother hadn't eaten more than a bite or two. I wrapped the pot pie in tin foil and put it back in the refrigerator in case she wanted it later.

When we got in the car, I waited for Skip to say something about the shabbiness of the place I'd come from. But all he said was, "Your mother's a hot shit," while I shook my head, thinking, *who knew*?

Two weeks later I received a call from Hospice. Skip had a car drive me down to Warwick, and I spent the last four days of my mother's life camped out between my old room and the hospital bed set up in the living room, marveling at how slowly death took a suffering person. I held my mother's hand constantly, but she waited until I was tucked under the pink chenille blanket in my old twin bed, napping, before she passed.

Tamara came to be with me, and Skip joined us for the memorial service.

"What the fuck?" she whispered to me when he walked into the chapel.

"I told you we were still dating," I reminded her.

"You've gone from fucking to dating to funeral attendance," she hissed. "This is *not* keeping it light, Eve. This is not doing it like a guy."

I shrugged.

"I'm not a guy."

I decided December was the absolute worst month of the year. Everywhere I went, it was all bright lights and cheer and merriment, while I was dealing with selling my childhood home, settling my mother's meager estate, and trying not to think too much about how alone I was in the world.

Skip tried to cheer me up – he even sent me lilies instead of roses, which I knew meant he was really trying – but I was in a funk I couldn't seem to shake myself out of, and worse, the entire world seemed to be conspiring to rub it in with their damn carols and Christmas bustle.

Then Skip got on the bandwagon. He arrived at my apartment with a Christmas tree he could barely fit through the door of my tiny apartment. He squeezed it into a corner and began stringing up lights.

"Mourning's over," he announced.

"It doesn't work that way," I countered.

"It does now. Go get cleaned up and dressed. You've been in that bath robe for three days straight."

I opened my mouth to object, then closed it. I showered and put on a clean sweater and jeans, and I pulled my hair up into a loosely-pinned pile atop my head. I swept some blush across my cheeks and put on earrings. It was the closest to human I'd looked or felt in a while.

"There's my girl," Skip said, gathering me into his arms when I emerged. I saw he'd brought ornaments, too, and had begun to hang them on the tree. "Don't you feel better?"

"I'm still an orphan," I said, then bit my tongue. I waited for him to laugh.

"Is that what it is?" he asked solemnly, pulling me to sit on the sofa beside him.

I nodded.

"I have no family," I whispered.

"Oh baby," he sighed, pulling me to him. "How about if I'm your family?"

I looked up at him quizzically. He pulled away and fumbled in his pocket.

"This isn't how I was going to do this, but…"

I looked down at the small blue box wrapped with a white satin ribbon.

"Go on," he said. "Open it."

The diamond sparkled in a Tiffany setting. If I'd known the first thing then about color, cut, clarity and carat, I'd have been too nervous to put it on my finger. As it was, I just held the thing there in my palms, still in the box. Skip had to extract it and slide it onto my ring finger.

"That's where that belongs," he said. "Marry me. I'll be your family. We'll start a family of our own."

Breathless, I nodded. He'd said the magic word three times in under five minutes: *family*. That was what I wanted, what I needed to keep me from feeling so horribly lost.

We made love on the sofa, the little white lights sparkling on the half-decorated Christmas tree.

Later, when Skip was snoring beside me, that I realized he hadn't exactly asked me if I'd marry him. He'd pretty much just told me I would.

In May, I finished law school, and in June I passed the bar. In early September, I married Skip on the lawn of his family's home in Newport. Kitty wore black.

"You look lovely, dear," she said, a note of surprise carefully emphasized. "I wouldn't have imagined anyone could look presentable in off-the-rack."

Tamara brought her new boyfriend, Howard, as her date. He was an artist and he dressed like one, with a flamboyant purple tie and more rings on his hands than Kitty wore. After her second martini, Tamara dragged me into the ladies' room for a confession.

"Aim that bouquet at me, Mrs. Wolcott. I'm smitten!"

When the time came for Skip and I to exit the reception, though, I couldn't find Tamara in the crowd. I scanned left and right, and then she appeared, sheepishly pulling Howard along behind her. Both of them had seriously-mussed hair, Howard's shirt was half-untucked, and he was wearing more of Tamara's lipstick than she was. I laughed and ran to her, hugging her fiercely as I handed her my bouquet of lilies and heather.

"God, I love you," I said, kissing her cheek. I kissed Howard's cheek, too, for good measure.

"Right back atcha, sister," Tamara said, squeezing my hand. She gave Skip a sideways glance and whispered, "He treats you right or I cut his dick off, okay?"

Skip and I honeymooned in Aruba, then moved into a rented house on the East Side of Providence. He went to work for his uncle's firm downtown. I found a job with a small firm on South Main Street, working in real estate law, much to Skip's amusement.

"I don't know how you stand the drudgery," he said to me, clearly delighted that he was no longer dealing with it.

But as it turned out, I didn't find it to be drudgery. Rhode Island, I quickly learned, was a bizarre little state. Instead of the county registries I'd become acquainted with in Massachusetts, each town maintained its own land evidence records, often with the system varying on the whim of the clerk in office. I loved the small towns, with their petty fiefdoms, quirky staff and musty vaults.

Better still, I was not the only new attorney starting out with the firm. Cara Perkins, a sassy short-haired brunette just about my age, had been there only two weeks when I was hired. She showed me the ropes (to the extent she'd learned them), and we became fast friends. I was thrilled when we were sent out on projects together. A trip to archives in rural Little Compton meant a meandering drive in her zippy Saab convertible, the top down in the late fall sunshine, and a stop at Four Corners Grille for lunch.

"We're having far too much fun," she would joke. "They're going to dock our pay."

I was just glad to finally have a girlfriend again. I missed Tamara, but she was teaching art classes in Connecticut and talking about taking over her parents' farm there, so I didn't expect she'd be living near me again any time soon.

Cara began coming out with me and Skip for after-work drinks, bringing along whichever guy she was seeing that particular evening. She seemed to be forever going out on first dates. We rarely saw the same guy twice.

And then, just as December rolled around and I began to dread the holidays and the anniversary of my mother's death, a wonderful thing happened. While I was hiding out in the ladies' room at work, wondering what I'd eaten the night before that had made me so queasy, Cara popped into the pharmacy up the road and returned with two small boxes.

"Here you go," she said, reaching into the bathroom stall. "Pee on the stick."

Minutes later, we were looking at two sticks, each with a clear plus sign.

"It wasn't something you ate," Cara said, hugging me.

I called Tamara, who shrieked, "No fucking way! A fucking baby?"

"Could we please not call it a 'fucking' baby?" I asked.

"Well, how the hell else did you get knocked up?" she teased.

I told Skip that night, over a dinner that included baby peas and baby red potatoes, though I don't think he quite got it. He seemed less than enthusiastic, and we finished our meal in silence. Skip retreated to the bedroom while I cleared the dishes. I crawled onto the bed behind him, spooning him and whispering in his ear.

"It's our family," I smiled. "It's starting, just like we talked about. Aren't you excited?"

"'Course I am," Skip said, turning and kissing me on the forehead. "I just didn't think it would happen so soon."

He turned his back to me again. I reached around, running my hand over his chest as I kissed the back of his neck. I slid my hand down between his legs and was startled to find that, for the first time in the history of my hand making contact with his crotch, he wasn't hard.

"Sweetie, I'm tired," he said.

I pulled my hand away and lay on my back for a few moments, staring at the ceiling and trying not to cry. Then I turned my back to him, cupped my hands over my belly and tried to feel some difference there, and I fell asleep.

I woke to overwhelming nausea the next morning, and was dismayed when it didn't pass as the day went on. I left work early every day for a week, then went to see my doctor. As it turned out, I had hyperemesis gravidarum – H.G., or extreme, never-ending 'morning' sickness – well before Kate Middleton made it a condition the world cared about. Cara brought me work to do at home, but I was often so ill I couldn't even sit up. Two weeks in, I'd lost so much weight that my doctor had me hospitalized and fed by I.V. I was miserable, and to make matters worse, Skip was working crazy hours. He would leave at 7 a.m. and I wouldn't see him again until 9 p.m. or later. "It's this case," became his refrain.

When my condition hadn't improved after a month, I took a leave of absence from work. Cara tried to keep me in the loop, stopping by at lunchtime to offer the latest in office gossip, but I felt rapidly more isolated. By the end of my first trimester, I was struggling with depression as much as good old H.G. I missed my life.

It was nearly the end of my second trimester before I felt any relief from the nausea, and at that point it seemed my office was getting by without me just fine. One of the partners suggested I just "relax" for the duration of my pregnancy and we could discuss my return once I'd had enough time at home with my baby. I'd already had enough time at home to last me a lifetime, but I supposed it would be different once the baby arrived.

My third trimester felt like a breeze compared to the prior six months. I was eating and getting out daily for walks, morning and evening. I had a belly that was discernably pregnant, and a little person doing somersaults within. The only problem was that Skip and I hadn't had sex since I'd told him we were expecting.

I tried to talk with him, but it was an exercise in frustration. There were excuses, and good ones: I'd been sick, he'd been overwhelmed at work. But the truth, I suspected, was this: I was fat and ugly and undesirable. My feet were swollen and my hands had gotten so puffy I couldn't wear my wedding and engagement rings any more. My wardrobe consisted of tent-sized dresses in the world's most unattractive fabrics and patterns, as designers had yet to catch onto the idea that pregnant women were still, ahem, *women*. I couldn't blame Skip for not wanting to touch me, but I couldn't make myself stop craving affection, either. I'd have given my left boob just to have him hold me and tell me I was pretty, even if it was a lie.

But Skip said and did no such thing, and my downward spiral continued. One week before my due date, as I left my doctor's appointment, I was feeling especially awful. I'd made the appointment in the evening so Skip could be there, but once again he was working. So I'd waddled, fat, alone and crying, across the darkened parking lot to my car. I wasn't far from Cara's condo, so I decided to stop by and cry on her shoulder.

If you can see where this is going, you're way ahead of where I was that night.

Somehow I walked right past Skip's car on my way to Cara's door. It didn't even register. And when I knocked and got no answer right away, even though I could see a light on in the living room? I still didn't get it.

It was only when I tried the door, found it unlocked, and let myself in that I understood. And even then, I was so damned naïve that it took me a minute. My first, split-second thought was that it wasn't unusual to see Skip and Cara together, and then my brain caught up.

It *was* unusual to see them together naked.

Skip was attempting to pull up his pants, which was apparently difficult with a raging hard-on, because he stumbled and hit the floor like a ton of bricks. And Cara? She stood there, stunned, giving me a full-frontal view of the woman I'd thought was my friend. The worst part was that it was like looking at the sun during an eclipse. I knew I should look away, but I couldn't. She was so thin and beautiful, with her flat stomach and her

119

slight hips and her perky breasts. There I was, roughly the size of the Hindenburg, with my swollen feet straining at the straps of my very un-sexy Birkenstocks. I just wanted the floor to open up and swallow me whole.

"Eve, I'm so..." Cara began, the words coming from her red-smeared mouth. I could guess where the rest of her lipstick had gone.

I held up my hand.

"Don't," I said. "Just don't."

"Eve, sweetheart," Skip said, having collected himself from the floor and finally zipped his pants.

"Don't," I said again.

I shook my head and I turned to leave.

And then suddenly there was warmth. My legs, my feet. I slipped on the tile and caught myself before I fell.

Holy shit, I thought. *I peed. I just pissed myself in front of my husband and his mistress.*

"Oh no, Eve," I heard Cara gasp.

"Eve," Skip said. "Sweetie, did your water just break?"

Oh no. It was worse than piss.

I turned around slowly. Cara and Skip stood frozen, wide-eyed, mouths gaping.

"Well, for chrissakes," I barked, breaking the silence. "Put some clothes on and get me to the hospital."

Cara reached for her dress, which was crumpled on the floor.

120

"Not you!" I cried. "Don't you come anywhere near me. Skip, are you going to drive me to the hospital or do I have to drive myself?"

Truth be told, I didn't want him anywhere near me, either, but I was feeling the first of what I presumed were contractions. Driving myself seemed like a bad idea, and I wasn't sure calling a cab was a better option.

Skip pulled on his shirt, grabbed his car keys, then stopped short.

"I can't drive," he said. "I'm pretty sure I'm drunk."

Fabulous. We'd had a car and driver in Boston, when we could have walked anywhere we liked, but now? I looked at Cara, who was wriggling back into her dress.

"How about you?"

She raised her eyes as if considering.

"Ah, one glass of wine..." she looked at the clock, "two hours ago."

"You win," I said, my knees buckling under the increasing pressure of the contractions. "Skip, give her the keys."

I sat in the passenger seat as Cara drove to the hospital. Skip perched in the backseat, his head between us.

"I really am so, so sorry, Eve," Cara said as she drove.

"Shut up," I replied.

I heard Skip open his mouth.

"You too," I hissed. "Not a word. You have no idea how lucky you are that I am in physical pain right now."

Eli was born at eight-fifteen the next morning. By then, Tamara had arrived and sent Cara and Skip packing with some harsh words and a threat or two involving removal of Skip's manhood. I held Tam's hand while I pushed, certain that there had been some sort of misunderstanding between me and my doctor; surely all my internal organs were coming out right along with this baby. But in the end, what I had wasn't a violent death but a perfect eight-pound baby. I also had my best friend in the world right there, telling me how strong and beautiful I was. She was lying, of course – I was a sweaty mess, swimming in a variety of bodily fluids, and I'd done some very un-strong crying and pleading for drugs – but I was okay with that.

Skip slunk in around ten, freshly showered and dressed and having been granted clearance to visit by Tamara, who guarded the doorway like a bulldog. I'd told her the only thing I couldn't deal with just then was Kitty.

Skip sat stiffly in a chair in the corner, holding a bouquet of wildflowers. He'd finally gotten the flowers right, though I'd have bet that was because that was all they had in the hospital gift shop. I nursed Eli at my breast, trying to keep negative thoughts at bay. Babies could sense that sort of thing, I'd read. I didn't want my little boy feeling as I did in that moment.

"Can I see him?" Skip said at last.

I nodded and he crossed the room. He seemed startled to find the baby attached to my nipple.

"You know, that's actually what they're for," Tamara shot from the doorway.

I laughed.

"I couldn't have screwed this up worse if I tried, could I?" Skip said.

I saw that his eyes were tearing up, but I was a long way from forgiveness.

"No, I don't think so," I said. "That was a world-class screw-up. Also probably the cruelest thing anyone has ever done to me."

Skip cried freely, then.

"Please, Eve. Give me a second chance, and I'll spend the rest of my life making it up to you, I promise."

"Listen," I said, keeping my voice soft for Eli's benefit. "I'm not making any big decisions just now. I'm a mass of hormones. Just do me a favor. Keep your mother away until I get home. I can't deal with her on top of everything else."

Skip nodded vigorously.

"Done," he said.

"Keep yourself away, too," I added. "Tam can call you when I'm ready to come home. For now, I'm trying to give this little boy a gentle welcome to the world, and every time I look at you, I want to kill someone. Understand?"

Skip nodded again, chastised.

"You broke my heart," I said quietly.

Skip started crying again. I closed my eyes and turned away.

"I love you, Eve," he said as he left.

"I know you think you do," I whispered after him.

People can adapt to anything. Take Stockholm Syndrome, in which individuals form a bond with their captors. It's a survival thing, and perhaps a bit extreme to relate to my situation, but ultimately I did decide to just move on and let Skip try to patch things up with me. I know how crazy that sounds, but at the time, I really couldn't think of a better option. I suddenly understood the notion of people staying together for the children. Every time I looked at Eli, I swore he deserved better than a single mother who would have to spend all her time working just to make ends meet. I also saw Skip in his features, and that brought me back to the image in my mind's eye of little four-year-old Skip running up the beach with jellyfish in his swim trunks. Doc Wolcott had doomed me with that story. It made me sympathetic to Skip, especially now that I had a little boy of my own. It made me more forgiving, perhaps, than I ought to have been.

We brought Eli home and pretended for family and friends that nothing was wrong. Only Tamara and Nate knew the truth, and though they both argued that I should divorce the bastard and move on, they eventually accepted that I wasn't going to do that just then.

Skip and I went to counseling and he jumped through flaming hoops to prove he'd changed. We bought the house in Jamestown and I imagined how it would feel to live there surrounded by children and family and friends. To have the kind of home I dreamed of as a child. The two years after Eli was born were a second honeymoon for me and Skip. He was sorry, I knew he was, and truth be told, I was relieved to let him make amends.

Then I found out I was pregnant again, and my anxiety and doubts returned. Pregnancy had driven us apart before. He hadn't been able to make love to me while I was carrying Eli, and look where that had led.

Skip anticipated my fears, though, and my second pregnancy was nothing like the first. I escaped the grip of H.G. and felt healthy from the start, and Skip made the extra effort to tell me I was beautiful. He treated me reverently, and yes, we did have sex. He even seemed to enjoy it.

The only complication came when we learned Max was breech. An attempt to turn him failed, so I had to deliver via C-section. The recovery was brutal, and it seemed every time I'd retreat to my bedroom for rest, Kitty would show up and stick a bottle in my kid's mouth, determined to ruin my efforts to breastfeed.

From there, though, we settled into our lives, one year flowing into the next. We adopted Sally, our giant Leonberger menace, and the boys chased her around the yard. We put in the

125

swimming pool, setting my mind at ease where the boys and the rocky shoreline was concerned. We hired a nanny to help with the driving and the housework. I took on volunteer assignments as Kitty offered them up.

When Skip announced that he'd been offered a job with a firm in Boston, it just seemed to make sense to have him spend weeknights in the Brownstone that had been in the Wolcott family for generations, while I stayed with the boys in Jamestown. I loved our home, and I had the nanny to help. Skip made an effort to work from home on Mondays or Fridays, extending his time with us.

And when those work-from-home days dwindled and then disappeared, I almost didn't notice. My life had become so busy, between the boys and maintaining the house and volunteering for everything under the sun. Sure, I needed some anti-anxiety medication for a while, and then my doctor added the antidepressants, but who didn't have a crutch of some sort? I didn't realize how far apart Skip and I had drifted until it was too late.

Skip's second affair (or the second affair that I knew of) began when Max was five and Eli seven. It was with a female attorney at his firm in Boston, and though I knew, I never confronted him. My therapist said this was "avoidance." I said it didn't seem like such a bad thing to me. If I suspected, that was one thing. But if I knew? Then what? Divorce? Upending our life with the boys? After a while I talked myself into believing I was just overly suspicious.

126

The years passed, and the evidence mounted. There was always some new female "friend" whose name would come up in conversations about his time in Boston. There were late-night calls, and then, when Skip acquired a cell phone and carried it with him everywhere, there were messages from unidentified numbers. There was a condom in his pocket once, though I'd had my tubes tied by then, and there were all those nights he was out late and headed straight for the shower when he got home.

Did I know? Of course I knew. I'm no idiot, though I may have tried to be. If you take enough Zoloft and keep yourself busy enough, the devil you know becomes an acceptable option.

Right up until your kids grow up and your in-laws herd them into boarding school.

Until the itch of being in your own skin becomes too much to bear.

Until the nanny's cheap pink lipstick sets you off on a fabulous midlife crisis.

Until you realize that the marriage you suffered to save was over many, many years ago.

Chapter **Six**

I woke, disoriented, from a dream of dancing with Skip at our wedding. It took me a while to remember where I was: in the hospital in Westerly, recovering from an attempt at eliminating my medication as dramatically as I was proceeding with everything else in my life of late.

The nurse I vaguely recalled was named Candy stood over me, another woman in scrubs at her side. The second woman was auburn-haired and appeared to be about Eli's age.

"I'm Dr. Carter," she said.

Clearly I'd misjudged.

"We need to talk," she continued, "about whether you feel you can do detox as an outpatient, or need to stay here in the hospital."

"Detox?" I asked, confused.

Dr. Carter nodded, while Candy left the room.

"Your husband told us you tried to give up your medication cold turkey?"

"My husband?"

Now I was really confused. Who'd contacted Skip?

Dr. Carter looked at the clipboard she was carrying.

"Phinneas Berwick?"

Finn.

"Oh," I said. "He's just…a friend."

Was it my imagination, or did some trace of amusement flicker across Dr. Carter's face?

Woman brought by ambulance from a hotel room.

Hot guy - not her husband - made the call.

Got it.

"Well," Dr. Carter resumed. "Your…*friend*…was he correct?"

"Yes," I said, feeling slightly stupid.

"As I'm sure you've realized now, that was a pretty serious cocktail of medications you were taking. You can't just stop taking them. You need to be weaned off gradually." She paused, pursing her lips. "Of course, the other issue is whether you should, in fact, be weaned off them, or if you truly need them. Those were heavy dosages of antidepressant and anti-anxiety meds. I've put in a call to your doctor for her input, but I'm curious. What made you feel you don't need them anymore?"

What could I say? For reasons I couldn't quite put my finger on, I felt as though I was waking from a deep sleep. As if the medication had numbed me to things in life both bad and good, yet something had prickled beneath the surface until I couldn't deny it any longer. I'd spent a dozen years as a human guinea pig, forever switching from one drug to another, trying to eliminate side effects and find the right dosage. But what if there was no right dosage? What if the reason I never felt fully better was that I was going about it the wrong way? What if I was masking the problem instead of solving it? I'd taken for granted that my life was structured a certain way, and that I just had to muddle along. *Don't rock the boat, Eve!* But I'd rocked it now, hadn't I? I'd behaved as no one would ever believe Eve Wolcott could, and I'd confronted Skip - however briefly - about behavior of his that had gone on too long. Maybe I was kidding myself. Maybe I really did need to be medicated. But something inside me was screaming that that wasn't the case. That medication might help me exist, but if I wanted to *live*, I had to do it without a row of amber bottles on my bathroom shelf.

I looked at the young woman in front of me, with her stethoscope and M.D. after her name, and couldn't think of a way to explain.

"It's okay," she said. "We've only just met, and I understand that these issues can be complicated. You don't have to - "

"I just..." I began, interrupting her. "I just want to be *me* again. And I'm not even sure I know who that is anymore."

Dr. Carter smiled sympathetically.

"We'll see what your doctor has to say when she calls, but for now, I'm stepping you down. That I.V. has about two-thirds your previous dosage. I'd like to keep you at least until tonight so we can continue to monitor your vitals, but then you should be able to do the rest as an outpatient if you like. Again, assuming your doctor agrees."

"Thank you."

130

"You have a visitor," Candy said from the doorway.

Finn entered the room as Dr. Carter made her exit. I could have sworn she winked at me.

Great. My midlife crisis as hospital cafeteria gossip.

"Hey," Finn said, taking a seat at the end of my bed. "I never thought I'd say this to a woman in a hospital johnny, but you look a lot better than the last time I saw you."

"Ha!" I laughed. I could only imagine what I looked like. "You must have a thing for basket cases. In the short time I've known you, you've seen me drunk, hung over, sick, and now hospitalized."

"For the record," Finn said, "you were most fun when you were drunk."

I grinned and shook my head.

"Seriously," I said. "There has to be an easier way for you to get laid."

"You know, I did have that thought," he mused.

We both laughed.

"My life just keeps getting more complicated by the minute," I observed. "The ultimate goal, I think, is to simplify, but in the meantime, it's going to get worse before it gets better."

"Yup," Finn agreed. "You've got more baggage than American Tourister."

"And you should do stand-up comedy."

He smiled devilishly.

Then he reached under the bedsheet, pulled my right foot onto his lap, and began to knead.

"Foot fetish?" I asked.

"I thought you could use a little attention."

"We were supposed to be a one-night stand."

"Were we?" Finn feigned shock. "Oh, that's right. You were going to just use me and toss me aside."

"Right," I teased. "But you seem to have an odd inability to let go. Must be some sort of damsel-in-distress syndrome? You like to be the rescuer?"

"I like you," Finn said. "You're smart and funny and I have the sense that what I've seen is only the tip of the iceberg, so to speak. I find that intriguing. And it doesn't hurt that even in a hospital johnny, you look eminently do-able."

I laughed so hard, I snorted. Most un-ladylike.

"You're very bad," I said. "And you probably should steer clear of me. Just leave me here in my hospital johnny and go find someone with less baggage. That Dr. Carter, for example. She looked 'eminently do-able,' don't you think?"

"Been there, done that," Finn said, deadpan.

"Seriously?" I cried, pulling my foot from his hands.

Finn laughed.

"Nope. Just kidding. I do know her from around town, though, and I'm not her type."

"How could you not be anybody's type?" I wondered. "Unless you're just too old for her."

Finn looked wounded.

"No! Too male, actually."

"Ohhhhh," I said. "So *I'm* more her type than you are!"

"Difficult as it is to believe," Finn said, pulling my left foot from under the sheets and beginning to knead. "There are actually some women who are impervious to my wit, charm, and good looks. Oh, and the penis. Impervious to the power of the penis. But baby, they were born that way."

Our laughter was interrupted by Candy, who came in with a scowl on her face.

"You're having too much fun in here," she said, and I couldn't tell if she was joking.

"Sorry," Finn apologized. "I was just about to leave."

I admit, I felt disappointed.

"Is there anything you need from your hotel room?" Finn asked. "I could pick some things up and come back."

"Really? You don't mind? I could use my phone and my iPad."

"Gotta check up on those rug rats, huh?"

His tone was teasing, but again I bristled.

"Yes, and I need to give my friend Wally a call. He'll steer me to a good divorce lawyer."

Finn stood and gave me a kiss on the top of my head.

"Good. I like the idea of you single."

"But you don't do long-term relationships, remember?" I said.

"True," he admitted. "But maybe a series of short-term relationships with the same woman is in order. You know, if I can convince her."

"No harm in trying," I smiled as he left.

Truthfully, though, I was beginning to feel I was in way over my head.

"Eve, I think you need to take 'Vacationing 101.' Hospitals are not involved."

I sat with my iPad propped against my knees, talking to Wally via Skype. He preferred Skype to phone calls because he was nearly deaf. "At least Skype gives me a shot at lip-reading," he'd say. So now, framed before me was his slender, slow-moving, octogenarian self. He was nearly bald, except for a thin layer of pure white hair combed carefully over his scalp. He wore round tortoiseshell glasses that he was forever pushing up on his nose. Having decided at 4:30 that his day was done, he was outfitted in navy pajamas with white piping and a plush maroon bath robe.

"You know me, Wally," I said. "Never a dull moment."

"You need to work on that," he said, and I agreed.

We chatted a bit more, and he gave me the names and numbers of two divorce attorneys he highly recommended. He didn't express surprise that I was divorcing Skip. In fact, I felt a silent approval from him. He wasn't gleeful at the news, but he seemed content with it.

"I'm proud of you, Eve," he said as we drew our conversation to a close. "The toughest thing in life is figuring out what you want. The second-toughest is going for it. You've done both already. It may seem rocky for a bit, but in the end I think you'll find smooth sailing ahead."

134

"Thanks, Wally," I said earnestly. "I hope you're right."

"You're on the right path, kid. It's like I always say. If you want hydrangea, you don't plant daisies."

I thought about that for a moment.

"That sounds true," I said. "Though in reverse, sort of. I've had the hydrangea. I want the wildflowers."

"Well," he said, his forefinger sliding his glasses up the bridge of his nose, "then you're definitely on the right track, kid."

I ended our call with a sense of calm and gratitude I hadn't felt before. That had to be a good thing, I imagined as I dialed Max. I got a text reply: *Busy. Talk later.*

I dialed Eli. I figured I'd get a similar response, but to my surprise, Eli answered.

"Hey, Mom."

"Hey, Kid. How are you?"

"Ducky," he said insincerely. "Peachy-frigging-keen."

"That bad, huh?"

"That bad."

"Are you going to give me details, or just let me go into Mom-mode and think the worst?"

A heavy sigh emanated from Eli's end of the line.

"Just the usual, really," he said. "I need to pick a sport, and I'm good at, oh, none. I need a social life, but 'smart' and 'social' don't really go together. A girlfriend would be cool, but I'm a major dork."

"Oh, kidface," I sighed. "Athletics aren't everything, a social life won't get you into Harvard, and eventually most girls figure out that dorks are the real hotties."

Silence from the other end of the line.

"E?" I asked, worried.

"I'm okay, Mom," he said, and he laughed a little bit, though the more I thought about it, the more it sounded as though he'd been crying. "You're funny, you know? I *wish* girls would figure out that dorks are the real hotties. Not holding my breath, though."

"I'm sorry, kiddo," I said. "You couldn't pay me to be your age again, but I promise you this: you just hang in there and it gets better."

"Really? Is it better for you?"

For a split second I felt as though I might as well be on Skype. Eli and I had always been close. I didn't doubt that he might be able to sense my distress as clearly as if he could see my hospital johnny and hollow eyes through the phone.

"It is," I said, willing myself to channel the optimism I'd felt in the wake of my chat with Wally. "It will be. I'm working on it. That's all life is. A work in progress."

"Sometimes it seems like it's just the 'work' part," Eli lamented.

My heart broke. Truly. I was sure I heard it splitting. I could remember delivering him from my womb like it was yesterday. I could remember cradling him and nursing him and imagining all the best for him. The despair in his voice was almost more than I could bear.

"I know," I said simply. "And I'm sorry. I don't think that's the way it's supposed to be." I paused, almost afraid to offer him what I wanted to say next. "Can you hang in there a little while? Could you do that if you thought there were other options?"

"What do you mean?" he said warily.

"Well, Morefield isn't the only school on the planet," I said. "What if there was another school that might be a better fit?"

Eli sighed as if exasperated by a small child.

"Haven't we talked about this before? Dad would shit a brick. Um, you know. Pardon my French."

"I know," I said, wondering if I'd gone too far off the deep end, yet unable to hold back. "But Dad's not your only parent. Just hang in there, okay? This might take a while, but if Morefield is not the right place for you, I think we can do better."

"Seriously?" Eli asked.

The hope in his voice almost crushed me, but it stirred something in me, too. That was my baby on the other end of the line. He nearly topped me in height these days, and he was awkward and moody and smelly, but he was my baby. I'd have wrestled a grizzly bear for him. Surely I could stand up to Skip. I felt shamed that I hadn't before.

"Seriously," I affirmed. "I can't make any promises just now, but I'm working on it, okay? Trust me?"

There was a pause.

"Okay," Eli said at last. "I trust you."

"I love you," I told him, choking back tears.

"Yeah. Ditto," he said, and then he was gone.

I sat in silence for a moment or two, then I dialed again.

"Hey, Howard," I said, silently glad that Tamara hadn't

answered. There was too much I didn't want to explain at the moment. "You're just the person I need to talk to. Eli's thinking of a change in schools, and I've heard that Pinecroft has a great art program. It's right in your back yard, so I thought you might know something about it?"

I might as well have asked him about Andy Warhol, his personal hero. Howard went on. And on. And on.

"And remember Matthias? My roommate at RISD? He's the head of school now," Howard concluded.

It was just what I wanted to hear.

"How soon can I get Eli an interview?" I asked.

"I'll set it up for Wednesday," Howard said. "You've really got Skip on board with this? I thought he was married to Morefield."

"I'll get him on board," I said, believing it for the first time. "Thanks, Howard."

I hung up and texted Eli.

Check this out. No sports requirement. They have independent study in the arts. Matthias Walter is head of school.

I added the link to Pinecroft's web site.

I had to wait less than a minute for Eli's response.

No way.

I smiled and tapped in my reply.

Way.

I'd kill to go there, Eli responded.

Please don't. I replied. *You have an interview on Wednesday. Murder is probably frowned upon.*

I looked at my screen for a full two minutes, wondering

138

what was going on in Eli's head. Then his response came.

You rock, Mom.

I was sitting in a hospital bed, wearing a johnny, my hair limp and my skin tacky with dried sweat.

My life was a train wreck and I'd just promised my son something that was going to mean an uphill battle with Skip and no end of shit from Kitty.

And I felt like a million bucks.

Chapter **Seven**

Though it sounds negligent, I first noticed Finn's set of
wheels on the drive back from the hospital. It wasn't the Porsche
or Maserati I expected. It wasn't even close. It was a 1969 Ford
F100 Ranger pickup, restored so beautifully it could have been a
time machine. Candy-apple red with two-tone leather interior.

"Are you kidding me?" I asked as I climbed into the cab.

"What?" Finn responded.

"This is you car? Your, um, truck?"

"Same one you rode in yesterday, and the night before
last," he clarified.

Yesterday, my main focus had been refraining from
vomiting on the short drive to Ocean Manor. I hadn't noticed
much beyond how awful I felt. But the night before last?

"Remember?" Finn prodded. "After the beach?" When I
gave him no hint of understanding, he went on. "When you
were a sloppy-drunk mess, and I took your keys, brought you
back to the hotel, and tucked you in. That night. Ring any
bells?"

I recalled waking up in my nightshirt, wondering how

that had happened.

"Oh," I said simply.

"So you don't remember Bessie here at all?" Finn asked.

"Bessie?" I laughed.

"Well, what the hell else do you name a truck like this?"

I continued laughing.

"It's the weirdest thing," I said at last, a vague memory tugging at the edges of my thoughts. "My dad had a truck just like this. Well, not this pristine, but same vintage. My mom thought it was a nightmare. She kept trying to get him to ditch it, trade it in on something she deemed acceptable. But man, was that a no-go."

I shook my head and chuckled.

"A man and his truck," Finn said. "What leverage did your mama think she had?"

"She'd clearly overestimated her powers," I conceded. "Still, I've gotta say, I'm kind of surprised. This can't be your only mode of transportation. What other cars have you got stowed away in your garage?"

"A BMW with all-wheel drive for the winter, and two MG's, all pulled apart like Dr. Frankenstein's been at 'em. Why?"

I shrugged.

"You've got so much damn money..."

"Ah, you expected a ride home in an Aston Martin?"

"Maybe a Maybach," I joked.

Finn grinned and shook his head. There was something about his silhouette there in the truck: his tanned wrists at the wheel, the cuffs of his chambray shirt, the glint of his battered stainless steel watch. Somehow, even though I knew he was made of enough money to drive anything he wanted, he fit with the timeworn whipstitched seats and the chrome-rimmed console.

"My boards fit just right in the bed," he said, nodding his head toward the back of the truck. "And there's more than enough room for a paraglider. I can toss in my tent, all my camping gear, head up to Burke for the weekend."

"They make new trucks, you know," I said.

"Not like this, they don't."

I couldn't argue.

"Hey," I said. He'd brought the truck to a stop in front of the gates to his house. "What about dropping me at the hotel?"

Finn let out a small sigh, as if he'd expected an argument and had prepared his rebuttal.

"You shouldn't be alone right now," he said. "I'll take you back to the hotel in the morning."

"Honestly, Finn, I'm fine. You heard Dr. Carter back there. They wouldn't have let me go if I wasn't."

The gates swung open and Finn pulled truck inside. We made our way slowly toward the house. A smattering of lights was on, their pale yellow glow reaching out into the night. I could see Oscar Wilde's pointy-eared silhouette in the front bay window.

"Non-negotiable," Finn said.

"You're kidnapping me, then?" I asked, an eyebrow raised.

"If I must. You didn't do a very good job of looking after

yourself the past couple of days."

I couldn't argue that point.

Finn parked the truck in the garage and I followed him through a series of corridors and up a small flight of stairs. We emerged into a hallway on the main floor of the house. Oscar Wilde circled my legs, purring.

"Are you hungry?" Finn asked. "You didn't eat much of your dinner at the hospital."

"Of course not," I laughed. "Did you see it?"

"So how about - I don't know - a grilled cheese or something?"

I shook my head and yawned. It was after eleven p.m.

"Really, I'm just tired," I told him sincerely.

Finn held up his index finger. He filled two glasses with water and set them on a tray. He added a small dish of crackers to the tray.

"Just in case," he said.

I marveled at his hospitality. Not the usual bachelor treatment.

He balanced the tray in one hand and took me by the other. I followed him up the stairs.

"I could use," I said hesitantly, sniffing at the cloud of hospital smell that still surrounded me, "a shower?"

Finn laughed.

"Well, I wasn't going to say it," he teased.

He led me into the master bedroom, setting the tray down at the bedside. A massive bed in white linen stretched out below a skylight of equal size. Stars twinkled above. Finn crossed the room and opened a sliding glass door. A light breeze drifted in, pulling the sound of the surf along with it.

"This is lovely," I said quietly.

"Just a minute," Finn said, and he disappeared through a doorway.

I heard running water, and the flicker of candlelight cast shadows out into the bedroom.

"All set," Finn said, emerging.

I padded into the master bath, which was larger, even, than the one in my own home. Candles were lit here and there, and they were all so perfectly positioned, my jaded self wondered how many other women Finn had seduced right here. My eyes went to the giant whirlpool tub, and I regretted the things I could so easily imagine Finn doing there.

"Here," he said.

I startled, realizing he was right behind me. I took the towel he offered, setting it down on the edge of the tub. I watched as he crossed the room to the shower, an open area with teak flooring running on an artful diagonal. Water fell lightly from the ceiling. Finn swept his hand through the mist.

"Should be just right," he said.

I nodded, waiting for him to leave so I could undress. But he had other ideas.

He crossed the room and unbuttoned my cardigan, then slid it from my shoulders and let it drop to the floor. His hands kept moving, settling lightly on my hips, then sliding my yoga pants down until they pooled on the floor at my feet. Instinctively, I stepped free of them. I stood there in my tee shirt

144

and panties, as painfully aware of the sudden throbbing between my legs as I was of the mess I must be after my time at the hospital. I wanted Finn to leave, but I also wanted him to stay. He proceeded slowly, pulling my shirt over my head and letting it drop. I stood there, my heart pounding, wearing only my thin cotton panties and feeling self-conscious in a way that somehow had an edge of bliss, and then Finn's hands were again at my sides. He slid my panties down to the floor, and I stepped free of them.

I walked into the spray of the shower all too aware that he was watching me. I closed my eyes and let the water run over me, then turned my back to the wall. Finn was not only watching, he'd taken a seat on the edge of the whirlpool tub as if I were giving him a show.

"Are you going to sit right there the whole time?" I asked, trying to sound indignant.

Finn nodded slyly.

"I thought I might," he said. "Just for your safety, of course. In case you felt dizzy or sick again."

"I feel fine," I told him. I almost said, *Just like myself again*, but that wouldn't exactly have been accurate. "Much better."

I let the water soak my hair and I reached for the shampoo. The damn throbbing between my thighs was getting worse. Being watched by Finn had turned a mundane routine into torture. Delicious torture, but still. A tiny little voice of self-doubt nagged at me, told me my tan lines looked funny, my ass was too big, my breasts too small, my curves located in all the wrong places. And now here I was, putting it all on display before this chiseled hunk of a guy. How could this even be happening? How could this be my life? I closed my eyes again and lathered my hair furiously, feeling the suds run down my body and imagining they provided some sort of flattering cover.

"You're beautiful," Finn said, almost as if he could sense my thoughts and wished to offer a kindness.

I tipped my head and pretended I hadn't heard him. I ran a soapy washcloth all over, catching a whiff of almond from the soap and thinking, *now I smell like Finn.* I felt the water running over me, rinsing, and then it stopped.

I opened my eyes and found Finn standing right in front of me, a towel opened to gather me in. I let him wrap me up, folding me into his arms, and then I felt his lips at my ear. I tipped my chin and his mouth closed over mine.

"You are so, so beautiful," he breathed.

"You've already got me naked, you know," I joked.

"And so, so bad at taking compliments," he added.

I tried to think of a witty response, but I had nothing. The truth was, compliments and I had been strangers for a while. This would take some getting used to. Not that I'd mind.

Finn startled me, suddenly scooping me up and carrying me into the bedroom. He lowered me onto the bed and pulled the towel away. The breeze from the open door raised goosebumps on my skin, but the sound of the surf and the smell of the salt air was heavenly. I drank it in while Finn began paying gentle, dedicated attention to the task of drying me. He blotted my hair with the towel, then trailed kisses down the side of my neck. He dabbed at my arms and ran his lips over my breastbone. He moved the towel lightly down the length of my body. He dried my feet and kissed my toes until I laughed. He dropped the towel to the floor and leaned over me, kissing my nose and my lips with a smile. He kissed my breasts and I felt my head swim. And then he was between my legs, parting them, and I shivered in spite of myself. I felt his tongue and was sure I would lose my mind, would come in an instant and be left wishing it wasn't over already.

But damn, Finn knew what he was doing, I had to give him credit for that. He was a tease in all the right ways. Every time I'd be nearing the edge, he drew back.

"You're killing me," I whispered.

He laughed, but this time it was a low and almost sinister sound. Bad Boy Finn. He was clearly pleased with himself.

I was pretty damn pleased with him, too.

"Oh, fuck!" I cried out at last.

In a split second he produced a condom from thin air, rolled it on, and was inside me. We clutched at each other, rolled dangerously close to the edge of the bed. I found myself on top, biting my lip and looking down at the sensuous point where our bodies disappeared into one another. *God, those abs.* I leaned in, my hands splayed across his chest, my fingers tracing the lines of his tattoos. I kissed him furiously as he came.

He relaxed into the pillows, eyes closed, and I caught myself. I was looking at him a little too tenderly, considering his features fondly, as if I really knew him.

I rolled to the side and tucked myself into the crook of his arm. I waited for the snoring. (It usually took Skip about two seconds.) But Finn seemed alert. He rolled onto his side, facing me.

"Sorry," he said. "I really did mean to just take care of you tonight."

"I think we can safely say you did just that," I smirked.

Finn let out an amused sigh. His hand smoothed my damp hair back from my forehead. My eyes closed instinctively at his light touch.

"You're really something," he said, his tone approaching disbelief.

I thought of a dozen snarky things to say, but somehow, I kept my mouth shut. I kept my eyes closed, too, and enjoyed the sensation of his fingertips so lightly grazing my temple. God, I was tired.

Tired, and then deeply, soundly asleep.

I woke with the light of a nearly-full moon shining on me through the wide skylight above and the sound of waves outside the open door making it seem as though I were on a boat. The bedside clock read 3 a.m. I sat up and looked out at the moonlight on the water. Finn slept soundly beside me, Oscar Wilde a fluffy feline ball at his feet, and again the surreal feeling crept in. I'd gone from my home, from my increasingly-claustrophobic life, to Ocean Manor and the bad behavior I'd undertaken there, and now here I was, with a man I barely knew sleeping beside me. All because I'd somehow morphed from mousy housewife into naughty wild woman in record-breaking time. It was a series of events I wouldn't believe could have happened if not for the fact that, well, I'd lived it.

The sheet I was tangled in dropped away, and I realized I'd fallen asleep nude. This was something Eve Wolcott never did. And frankly, there was still enough of the old me left to feel this was an issue. I thought of my clothes where they lay on the bathroom floor, emanating hospital-smell. I wriggled out of the bed, briefly disturbing Oscar Wilde. I scratched him between the ears as I made my way to the bedroom closet.

It felt a little bit like snooping, poking around in Finn's closet while he slept. Maybe it *was* snooping. A small part of me wondered as I pulled the doors open just what I might find inside.

But if Finn had skeletons in his closet, they weren't here. All I could see here was a neatly-arrayed wardrobe comprised primarily of jeans and shirts, board shorts and tees. I spotted a lone suit and pair of dress shoes in the corner. I found a tee shirt that looked long enough to meet my nightshirt requirements, and I pulled it on.

I closed the closet door gently behind me and started back to bed. Passing the open door where the night air stirred the curtains, though, I felt the need to step out onto the balcony. Finn's tee shirt was little protection against the chill of the night air. I shivered and wrapped my arms around myself as I leaned against the railing.

The coastline here was rocky and undulating, dipping into small coves here and there. I could see the lights of Ocean Manor, and Finn's small sandy beach below. And as I looked to the right, I could see that I wasn't the only one awake at this hour.

On the patio of the massive mansion next door, a long, lean blonde reclined in a lounge chair, her back to me. She was scrolling through her phone, and it was the light of it that had first caught my eye. Then a sound reached my ears, so quiet beneath the lap of the waves and the crash of surf on sand that I nearly missed it.

She was crying.

I stood there and wondered if she was who I thought she was, the pop star nearly half my age. I wondered if she was crying for one of the lost loves she'd written a song about, or if she was crying because her life wasn't quite what she expected it to be. I thought of the reasons I'd cried at that age, and realized that marrying fairly young had rendered my life too different from that of a single pop star to even warrant comparison. She might have been crying over a failed album, or a tabloid story, or a boyfriend who didn't text back, or even just the fact that she couldn't go anywhere without bodyguards and an entourage. I'd cried over a difficult pregnancy, having to quit my first law job, and sitting home with postpartum depression while my husband 'worked late.' Apples and oranges.

And yet I couldn't help but feel a twinge of sadness for

the girl, couldn't help but think that, on some level, I understood. Who among us knew themselves fully at age twenty? Who didn't look back and think of all the naiveté, all the petty worries and burdensome assumptions, and feel a bit of sympathy for those going through it now? Who would want to go through that whole awkward, awful, magical, roller-coaster period of life in front of the entire world?

"Hey," Finn said, momentarily startling me. "Sorry. Didn't mean to scare you."

He stepped behind me and wrapped his arms around me.

"Geez, you must be freezing," he said, rubbing my arms. "Come back to bed."

The blonde girl next door looked around, as if she'd heard us but wasn't sure where the sound was coming from. I watched her get up from the lounge chair and return to the house. I let Finn take me by the hand and lead me back inside. He closed the door behind us.

"Couldn't sleep?" he asked as we settled back into the pillows and Finn tucked the covers over us.

"I needed a night shirt," I said.

"I see you found one," he smiled. "It looks much better on you."

"Thanks," I said, and then for no reason I could identify, I began to cry.

"Hey, hey," he said, pulling me into his arms. "What's the matter?"

He smoothed my hair back from my face and wiped at

my tears with his thumbs.

"I'm so sorry. I don't know, really. I mean, I kind of know - my life is a mess - but I don't know why I'm crying right now, exactly."

"Your life's not a mess," Finn said gently.

"It is," I argued. The floodgates had opened. "My marriage is a wreck, and aside from one very short phone chat confirming he's screwing the nanny, my husband won't even talk to me. My kids are in boarding school, one very happily, the other very *un*happily. And what am I? I'm a stay-at-home mom with no kids at home. A housewife without a husband. A lawyer with a whopping six months of practice under my belt a whole fifteen years ago and not a single goddamned marketable skill acquired since. I mean, what am I thinking, divorcing Skip? What the hell am I going to do?"

Finn sat in silence, stunned, probably, but I just didn't care. I waited for him to show the crazy woman the door.

"Listen," he said at last. "I'm probably doing the dumb-guy thing here, trying to fix the problem when you just want me to listen, but here goes. All your concerns are valid, but there's something else in play here that I think you should keep in mind. Twenty-four hours ago you were in the hospital because you'd tried to detox from some serious drugs. That's a shock to your system. Now you're on a stepped-down dosage of stuff your body has relied on for years. And this is all happening while you're going through some major stuff in your life. Of course you're going to feel mixed up. Of course you're going to need a good cry now and then. But keep in mind that some of what you're feeling is probably biological, some is situational, and all of it will pass. Cut yourself some slack."

I looked at Finn and bit my tongue. God, he was infuriating! Yes, he was totally doing the dumb-guy thing, trying to fix the problem when all I wanted was a shoulder to cry on. But worse? He was right. As much as part of me wanted to haul off and punch him, the greater part of me felt calmer already. I had decided to get off the antidepressants and anti-anxiety meds, and I really believed that was the right choice for me, but it wasn't going to be easy.

"Eve?" Finn said cautiously.

"Were you a shrink in a previous life?" I asked, trying to sound light, teasing.

"Sort of," Finn said. "My, ah, I knew someone who had some issues. Bipolar."

His words were unusually clipped. Clearly he wasn't going to say more on the topic, but my curiosity was piqued. Maybe it was that part of me that was all-girl and just couldn't refrain from trying to psychoanalyze a playboy like Finn. Or maybe - even worse - it was that I was truly interested.

I felt Oscar Wilde rise from his corner of the bed and tuck himself neatly into the curve behind my knees, purring.

"Oscar Wilde," I mused. "Why Oscar Wilde? He's kind of an odd figure to relate to."

"*The Picture of Dorian Grey*," Finn said. "It was probably the only book I read in college that stayed with me. I thought it was such a brutal, fascinating idea, to see your sins manifest physically on an image of yourself, while you stay young. As if someone else takes the punishment for all you do. Of course, in the end, you're still accountable."

I squinted at Finn, as if by looking hard enough I might see the meaning behind his words.

"It's such a dark story, though," I said, "and Wilde's life seemed so sad. You don't seem dark, or sad. Just the opposite. I can't quite figure the attraction."

"That's because you're reading too much into it," Finn said, the usual lighthearted inflection returning to his voice. "Everyone has their dark times, Eve. Maybe for me adrenaline is my antidepressant. I surf, I ski, I paraglide. I travel and wine and dine. I move too fast for sadness to catch up."

I thought about that, the idea that a person could outrun his sorrows. I wasn't sure I bought it.

"That's an interesting philosophy, Mr. Berwick," I yawned.

"Ah, yes! I can see my conversation is keeping you riveted."

"It's nearly 4 a.m.," I said in my defense.

"That it is," Finn conceded. "What the hell are we doing awake?"

I laughed and leaned into his chest. I still felt a bubble of sadness within me, threatening to rise, but at the moment, I was grateful for the distraction Finn provided. As long as I was with him, I was worlds removed from my own life, which was rapidly becoming a bumpy ride. This was escapism, but I was okay with that. I was cutting myself some slack.

Finn tipped my chin up and kissed me.

I intended to say goodnight and go to sleep, but as I was quickly learning, my intentions and my actions were two very different things when Finn was around. We displaced Oscar Wilde and took over the bed, rolling around in lazy, half-asleep kisses and caresses, before finally dozing off. My last conscious thought was that I seemed to have lost the tee shirt I'd borrowed from Finn's closet.

Finn couldn't have slept more than an hour. When I woke, I found my clothes freshly laundered and folded at the end of the bed. The bedside table held the bottles with my new prescriptions, as well as one tall glass of water and another filled with some sort of green smoothie-type beverage. I sat up and stretched, then searched beside the bed for my purse and pulled my phone out.

Max had sent more texts with links to lacrosse gear he wanted.

Eli had sent a photo of a Morefield cross-country shirt, which I gathered meant he'd reluctantly chosen his sport. He'd also included the letters "FML," which I would have to look up.

Tamara had texted: *Still having fun? Call/txt when u come up for air. Say hi to fuckbuddy Finn 4 me.*

Nothing from Skip, but I was getting used to that.

"Good morning, sleepyhead," Finn said, coming into the

bedroom from the balcony.

He was wearing nothing but boxer shorts slung low on his hips. I may have actually licked my lips. *Christ, those abs were going to kill me.*

"'Morning," I said, trying to smooth my hair and gather the bed sheet about me somewhat attractively. I was going for 'Greek goddess,' but suspected I was coming across more like Kristen Wiig in *Bridesmaids*.

"Drink your breakfast," Finn said, sitting down on the edge of the bed.

"What is it?" I asked, sniffing.

"Fruit, kale, yogurt, soy milk, and a little bit of almond butter."

I wrinkled my nose.

"It's good for you," he said. "And I promise it tastes good, too."

I took a sip. He wasn't lying. I wouldn't have guessed something that looked like this could taste so…well…not bad, anyway. I took my pills and washed them down with water, then finished the smoothie.

"So, what are we doing today?" Finn asked. "Surf lesson? The wind's picked up, and there are some waves out there."

"Let a girl wake up first?" I suggested, yawning.

"You're missing a beautiful day."

I looked at the clock. Damn, he was right. It was nearly 10 a.m. already.

"You should have woken me up."

"I thought you needed the sleep."

True.

Oscar Wilde swished into the room from the balcony. He hopped on the bed and began rubbing against me.

"I still don't get that," Finn said, watching the cat and shaking his head. "He usually doesn't like women."

"I'm very likable," I grinned.

"That you are."

Finn leaned in and kissed me on the nose.

"Don't get me started," I warned.

"Really? That's all it takes? Damn, woman, you're easy."

I cringed. That was actually quite true where Finn was concerned. I turned my back to him and disappeared into the bathroom to change before I could get into more trouble. Once dressed, I poked around the bathroom cupboards. I found some mouth wash to gargle with, and a brush I pulled through my hair. It still looked like a rat's nest, as it always did when I went to sleep with it damp, but it would have to do for now. All my hair products - not to mention my makeup - were back in the suite at Ocean Manor.

"I have an idea," Finn said as I emerged from the bathroom. "Let's go pick up your things from Ocean Manor, settle your bill, and you can stay here for the duration. Surf lesson this afternoon, a couple lobsters al fresco for dinner..."

"Didn't you already pitch this idea to me?"

"Yes, but you like me much better now," Finn said.

I couldn't help but laugh. It was true. I liked him better. Too much better. I had yet to file for divorce from Skip and here I was, putting my feelings on the line for a guy who'd told me up front that he didn't do long-term relationships. But then, the theme of the week seemed to be saying, "fuck it."

"Okay," I said.

"Okay?"

I nodded.

"I'd tell you no more funny business," I said, thinking again how odd it was to be flirting, and how very much fun, "but I'm beginning to think that's what I like best about you."

Finn smiled his killer smile.

"Come on," he said. "I'll go with you and help with your things."

I almost protested, imagining the gossip it would cause for me to pack up my belongings and leave with Finn Berwick. Then I remembered that I'd already made a slight scene, leaving the hotel by ambulance the other night. Tamara and I would just have to find another hotel for our girls' getaway in the future.

Finn and I walked the short distance to Ocean Manor. When we entered my suite, I marveled that it seemed like ages since I'd been there. I felt I was gaining distance from my life by degrees. As we collected my belongings, I wondered who I was becoming, and if it was less – or more – myself. Finn loaded my car as I settled the bill, and trusty Caleb gave me a sly glance as I headed out. I slipped him a hundred-dollar bill.

"See you next summer, Mrs. Wolcott?" he asked.

I thought about it for a moment and shook my head.

"Probably not," I said. "But thank you for everything. Stay out of trouble."

158

"Now, what fun would that be, Mrs. W?" he winked.

An hour later, my car was parked in Finn's driveway, my bags were in his bedroom, and we were in swim suits, loading surf boards into the back of his truck.

"Ready?" Finn asked, sliding into the driver's seat.

"As I'll ever be," I said.

I climbed into the truck and he patted the seat next to him. One glance at his bare chest and those abs was all the encouragement I needed. I slid over. He tipped his head and leaned in lightly, his nose and lips running faintly from the nape of my neck to the tip of my ear.

"You could cause an accident," he said.

"Good thing you haven't put the truck in gear yet," I smiled.

He laughed and sat up straight, trailing his hand along my thigh, which promptly went up in flames.

"Surfing," I said. "You're taking me surfing."

I hoped the water was cold. I was going to need it.

We drove a short distance to get to a beach he promised would be best for a beginner surf lesson. Unfortunately, it also meant we didn't have the privacy his beach afforded us. I scanned the shoreline as I zipped into my wetsuit. There weren't a lot of people, but enough that it was going to be embarrassing when I fell.

"You'll forget about them in five minutes," Finn promised, reading my mind. "We'll start on land."

He laid a surf board on the sand and I followed his instructions, stretching out on my belly on top of it.

"That's it," he said. "You want that line to run down the center of your body, and get your toes back there on the sweet spot. When you get a wave, you're going to get up. Hands come under your chest, elbows close. Lean back onto your knees. Bring that foot forward, and stand so the line is matched up with the arches of your feet. But keep your knees soft. Otherwise you'll be thrilled for one second, and in the drink the next."

I felt like I was playing Twister. There was no way in hell I was going to remember all this in the water.

"It's more intuitive than it sounds," Finn said, again reading my mind. "Come on, let's get out there and have fun."

"What about sharks?" I asked as we paddled out.

I was suddenly keenly aware that, prone on the board with my hands in the water, I'd look just like a seal from below. Shark food.

"No sharks here," Finn said.

I laughed.

"Right, because there's an invisible fence keeping them out of this part of the ocean?"

"Exactly. Now turn the board and get paddling. Here comes a good one."

I fell approximately six million times. Finn was right, though: if I had an audience on the beach, I didn't care. I came up sputtering and thrilled each time.

And then, when I'd passed the point of hoping I'd ever stand up on the board, I did.

"Oh my god, Finn, look!" I cried.

160

In my excitement, I stood up fully, forgetting to keep my knees soft. I caught a glimpse of Finn's face, amused, and then I was in the surf, the ocean tumbling me before spitting me out. I stood up in the shallows on shaking knees, grinning widely. Finn hugged me to him.

"You okay?"

"The best," I beamed at him.

"Better than sex?" he asked, nipping at my ear. Somehow he smelled even better all salty and wet.

"Don't be ridiculous," I grinned. "But this is the most fun I've had with a wetsuit on."

We paddled back out and spent another hour chasing waves. I stood up only two more times, but it didn't matter. I understood how Finn could lose an entire day out here. I felt as if I was finally part of the mysterious ocean world I'd found compelling my whole life, as if I had become one of the creatures I always wondered about when I gazed at the water's surface. I was salty and sandy, my fingers and toes wrinkled, and my muscles were giving me a preview of the ache I'd feel fully in the morning – and I couldn't remember feeling happier.

I realized on the drive back to Finn's what I mess I must be. My hair was a wild, flyaway tangle, and salt and sand had dried to a crust on my skin. I looked over at Finn and realized he didn't look bothered by my appearance at all. In fact, he looked… hungry.

Once in the driveway of his house, though, he banished me while he cleaned and put away the boards.

"Go on, take a shower. I'll take care of this."

"You're not going to join me?" I asked, disappointed.

Finn looked at his watch.

"I'm going to walk down to the dock and pick up lobsters for dinner, and I need to get there in the next half-hour. That won't happen if I follow you into the house."

That was true.

I went upstairs and checked my phone for texts from the boys, but there was nothing. I'd given up wondering if I'd hear from Skip. At this point, I was hoping I wouldn't. I'd have to deal with him soon enough, and in the meantime, I had thoroughly warmed up to my escape into this other world. Finn's world, where I was looked after and entertained, instead of always having to look after and entertain other people.

I texted a few quick lines to Tamara, telling her about my surfing adventure.

She responded immediately.

So he's well hung & can teach u 2 hang ten, 2? Go Red Fox GO!

I shook my head, laughing.

You are so bad, I texted, then swiped my phone shut and dropped it back into my purse.

I dug through my luggage and found a pale blue sundress, short and with a halter neckline. I set it out on the bed, then went into the Master bathroom and stepped into the shower. I peeled off my swimsuit as the warm water ran over me. The smell of the ocean rose from my skin, slowly replaced by the light almond scent of the soap. Finn's soap. Finn's scent. I couldn't help but recall my last shower here, with him as my audience. At the memory, I leaned my head back into the spray, my hands trailing down over my belly and between my thighs.

"I can't leave you along for five minutes, can I?" Finn said.

My eyes snapped open and my face flushed with embarrassment. He stood just outside the open shower, a wicked grin on his face. My hands went to my sides.

"Oh no, please," he said. "Don't let me interrupt."

"I thought you were going to get lobsters," I said, certain my complexion had turned the color of the unfortunate creatures we'd be eating for dinner that night.

"I did. I don't know what you've been doing this whole time," he said, then paused, the wicked grin returning to his face. "Well, maybe now I do."

I turned my back to him and reached for the shampoo.

"Let me," he said, and a few short moments later I felt him step into the shower behind me.

He lathered my hair, massaged my scalp. I was stunned by how sensuous it was, feeling his hands in my hair. Somehow it seemed his fingers were touching every nerve ending in my body. I leaned into him, feeling his chiseled chest against my back.

"There," he whispered in my ear.

He smoothed my hair down my back and I turned. I reached for him and he put my hand back at my side. He kissed my lips gently.

"Later," he said. "I want to sit next to you at dinner tonight and know you are thinking about sex every bit as much

163

as I am."

I considered the throbbing between my legs, the longing. *That's a safe bet*, I thought, but I said nothing.

He steered me out of the shower, in the direction of a towel he'd set down with a bottle of Gatorade on top.

"Hydrate," he said, catching me looking at the bottle quizzically. "You don't think of it when you're in the water all day, but you need to hydrate. That's a lot of sun and exercise we got."

I wrapped myself in the towel and took a long drink from the bottle. I couldn't help but look at Finn, the water running over his body, the tattoos wrapping his muscular, glistening wet arms. Even his tan lines were sexy. I left the room before I could frustrate myself any further.

A short while later I was dressed in my blue dress, perched on a bar stool at the island in Finn's kitchen, a glass of sublime organic chardonnay before me. From the speakers that seemed to be located throughout the house, an eclectic playlist drifted quietly: James Taylor, Chris Isaak, Norah Jones. A breeze drifted in through the doors that opened onto the deck, where Oscar Wilde lolled in the sunset. Before me, Finn was busily at work, preparing a salad and potatoes and waiting for the water in the lobster pot to come to a boil. I'd been told to sit still and stay out of the way.

It was fine by me. After a lifetime of preparing meals –
often at one time of evening for Eli and Max, then again
whenever Skip came home – I was only too happy to sip my
wine and watch Finn work. He was dressed in blue jeans and a
light gray tee shirt that fit him well. His bare feet danced across
the bamboo floor, moving from the refrigerator to the stove to
the cutting board. I could have watched him all night.

When it came time for the lobsters to go into the pot, I
excused myself and joined Oscar Wilde on the deck. I'd eaten
lobster my whole life, but I'd never killed the poor things myself.
I didn't want to be party to it now. I rubbed Oscar Wilde's belly
and sipped my wine, looking out over the water.

"The dirty deed is done," Finn said, appearing in the
doorway. "Just a few minutes now and dinner will be ready."
He paused, apparently noticing the lovefest between me and
Oscar Wilde for the first time. "He's letting you rub his belly?
Seriously? He doesn't even let me do that."

I shrugged.

"I must have the touch," I said.

"I'll say," Finn said, sotto voice.

He disappeared back into the kitchen and I followed.

"Shall I set the table?" I offered.

Finn shook his head.

"It's set," he said.

I looked at the empty dining room table.

"It is?"

"Not that one. I thought we'd eat outside. In the
pavilion on the dock."

165

I looked out toward the water again and realized there was a table in the center of the pavilion and little white lights beginning to twinkle in the gathering dusk.

"Good thinking," I said, slightly in awe. "Do you have a tray, then? I'll start taking things down."

Finn smiled.

"No need. Check this out."

He opened one of the kitchen cupboards and took out what appeared to be a large stainless steel box. He loaded the food into the box – steamed lobsters and all – and replaced the box in the cupboard.

"Watch," he said, pointing at the wall of glass at the back of the house.

He pressed a button and my jaw dropped. The box containing our dinner was working its way down a zip line to the pavilion.

"You've got this setup and you expect me to believe it's been two years since you got laid?" I asked, raising one eyebrow.

"I didn't say I hadn't had the opportunity," he replied. He picked up a bottle of wine and tucked it under one arm, then extended his other hand to me. "Come on. Let's go catch up to our food."

We made our way to the pavilion, Oscar Wilde following at our heels. When I saw the table, set as though for a formal dinner, complete with flowers and candles waiting to be lit, I turned my eyes to Finn.

"How did you do all this? I mean, when?"

"Okay, confession time," he said. "I hate to burst your

bubble, but I'm not perfect. Close and all, but there are some things I just don't do. I don't vacuum, for starters. Don't even know where in the house the thing is located. I do, however, have an excellent housekeeper, Carla, and she is sometimes willing to come in and do a little extra here and there. So today, while you and I were playing in the waves, Carla was here getting this ready."

I took a seat and lifted the wine glass Finn filled for me. "Here's to Carla," I said.

We clinked glasses. Finn took a sip, then set his glass down and turned to a panel behind him. He pressed a button and the floor beneath our feet began to vibrate as the deck floor had when Finn showed me his unique surf and paddle board storage system. I looked down and watched, mesmerized, as the planked floor in front of the table opened to reveal glass beneath. Finn pressed another button and the dark water was illuminated with light.

"Another one of your inventions?" I laughed, amazed.

"Yeah. I stayed in this glass-bottomed place in Tahiti once, and I thought it would be cool to recreate here. The water's not as clear here as it was there, but the lights draw some fish in at night. Once I figured out the board system, the mechanics of this were pretty easy. It was getting it past Coastal Resources Management that was the tough part."

"I'll bet," I said, recalling the trouble we'd had installing our swimming pool at the house in Jamestown.

Finn shifted his attention to unpacking our dinner while I peered through the glass at the water below. Oscar Wilde sat at the edge of the glass, his tail twitching as he looked down.

"He never gets tired of that," Finn remarked.

"I never would, either," I said.

A massive striped bass swam past, startling me.

"There are some big fish in there," I commented.

"That's nothing," Finn laughed. "It's pretty cool to see what we're swimming with. And pretty crazy sometimes."

I drew back from the glass and saw that dinner was ready. I also realized there was an entire lobster sitting on my plate. All the lobster I'd eaten had been previously disembodied. I loved lobster salad, lobster Newburg, lobster sautee...but this? I noticed Finn starting on his salad and happily began there.

"So, where did you grow up?" I asked him. "The more I get to know you, the more I'm picturing some wild, globetrotting childhood."

Finn laughed loudly.

"Nope," he said. "Not even close. Pretty boring, actually. I grew up in a Cape in a subdivision in Barrington."

"You're joking!" I cried, thinking of the sleepy bedroom community. "Boring-ton? You grew up in Boring-ton?"

Finn shrugged.

"What can I tell you? I wished it were more exotic even then. That's probably why I've traveled as much as I have, done all the crazy things I've done. I knew from about age eight that I didn't belong in a cul-de-sac."

"How about your parents?"

"Oh, they definitely belonged in a cul-de-sac," Finn

laughed. "Very traditional. My dad worked, Mom kept house. I got the feeling, though, that they hadn't exactly planned to have a kid. Or maybe they had, and then it turned out to be a different deal than what they'd expected. They weren't into it. I was always in the way of something. They weren't bad parents, but they weren't very good ones, either." He took a sip of his wine. "I guess that's why I never wanted to have kids. I figured I had no idea what to do, and I'd just screw it up."

I thought of that and felt a little twinge. I couldn't imagine my life without Eli and Max. I couldn't imagine not wanting children. And now, if I was honest with myself, I couldn't imagine how it would be when this – whatever it was – was over with Finn. Yet it seemed, if kids weren't part of the picture for him, there was no chance of this being any more than a passing fling. I tried not to think about it.

"Your parents?" I asked. "Are they…?"

"Alive and well," Finn affirmed. "Living in a condo in Scottsdale, Arizona and playing golf every morning. I see them at Christmas, and that's pretty much it. We don't have a whole lot to talk about."

"Funny. That's kind of like me and my parents," I said, taking a sip of wine, then laughing. "Well, mine have been dead for a while now, so that would be the reason we don't talk, but what you said before. About having the feeling they hadn't intended to have a child. I always had that sense with my parents. With my mother, at least. My father seemed a little more 'into it,' but he worked so much, he wasn't around often."

I didn't add that it had made me feel just the opposite of

how Finn felt, that it had left me with a longing for children and family. I speared a bite of my salad, delicious baby spinach leaves wilted by grilled asparagus and topped with stilton and balsamic vinaigrette. I'd watched Finn make it, and yet I couldn't believe this beautiful man had so damn many talents.

"So, can I just ask the blunt question?" he began. "How did a sweet girl like you end up with the jerk you married?"

I covered my mouth, as I was now laughing with it full. I gulped my salad down and then told him. I stuck with the greatly-abridged version, but I told him everything. I tried to avoid demonizing Skip. I knew anyone who'd stayed in such a marriage as long as I had needed to share the blame. When I finished, Finn looked at me and shook his head.

"I'm not sure if I'm supposed to say this or not," he said, "but Skip Wolcott sounds like a gigantic asshole. I don't understand how or why you stayed with him so long, but I hope like hell you follow through with the divorce, and soon."

Though he kept his voice even, something bubbled beneath the surface of his words. I wondered if it was anger, and if so, if it was directed at Skip, or at me. Finn started on his lobster while I sat for a moment, contemplating. I sipped at my wine and watched a school of minnows shimmer past the glass while larger, darker shapes moved below. Oscar Wilde appeared unmoved. He'd settled into a comfortable crouch, his tail twitching without any urgency.

I realized Finn had made short work of his lobster, while mine still sat there on my plate, staring at me with its dead eyes. I stared back. Finn noticed.

170

"Wait a minute," he said. "Don't tell me that after living in Rhode Island all this time, you don't know how to eat a steamed lobster?"

"I do," I said defensively. "In theory, anyway. I've always just had them...prepared. That's sitting there on my plate looking at me like a giant bug or something."

"Well, I'll be sure to give my compliments to the chef," Finn joked.

"I'm sorry," I said sincerely.

"Come over here," Finn said.

He slid my plate from its place at the opposite side of the table and set it alongside his. When I stood, he pulled my chair around, too. I sat next to him and watched as his hands went to work on the lobster. He twisted the tail and pulled the meat out, then tore it into smaller pieces. He dipped a piece into drawn butter and slipped it into my mouth, his fingers lingering there on my tongue. When he withdrew them, I barely had to chew. The lobster was so soft, it practically melted.

"That's delicious," I said.

Finn reached out with his thumb and wiped butter from the corner of my mouth. Then he leaned in and kissed me.

"You're delicious," he said, his nose to mine.

And just like that, it was thighs-in-flames time again. He must have been able to tell, because he drew back, settling that satisfied gaze of his on me once again.

"No dessert until you've had your dinner, Eve."

He proceeded with dismantling the lobster, feeding me

bite by bite. Butter dripped down his hand, and I licked it from his fingers.

Dear god, I was ruined for lobster rolls.

I wasn't even sure I'd finished my entrée until Finn pushed my plate toward the center of the table. He took his napkin and dabbed at the corners of my mouth, then covered my lips with a kiss. A new sort of hunger rose within me, reminiscent of our first, frenzied encounter on the beach. Only now I was sober; I hadn't drunk nearly enough wine to point a finger of blame there. Now it was all me, all my response to this animal feeling in the pit of my belly. I clutched at him, consumed by want.

Finn stood, scooping me up and carrying me away from the table. He laid me down on the glass floor of the pavilion and began undressing me. My halter dress unfastened easily, and he pulled the top down, exposing my breasts to the night air. One more deft tug and he'd removed the dress entirely. Beneath me, the glass was cold, and I could hear the lap of the waves, could feel the movement against the dock. Above, little white lights twinkled in the pavilion and danced in the sky beyond. I caught a glimpse of Oscar Wilde as he sauntered away, clearly perturbed that we'd taken over his spot.

Finn pulled a blanket from one of the chairs and tried to wrap me in it. I pushed it aside and pulled him down to me. It wasn't comfort I wanted. I pulled his tee shirt over his head, unfastened his jeans. In the chilly night, I folded Finn over me, warmer than the blanket he'd offered. With the sea below us, the stars above, and the night all around, I took him in – taste, touch, smell.

"Finn," I breathed.

But all I heard then was the lap of salt water at the glass, the crash of waves on the beach.

I woke to a phone call from an unfamiliar number.

It took me a moment to find my phone, to remember, even how Finn and I had ended up back in his bed after dinner...and dessert.

"Mrs. Wolcott? This is Caleb? From Ocean Manor?"

The cobwebs cleared slowly.

"Caleb, of course," I said. "Did I leave something?"

"Um, not exactly. There's someone here. Claims she knows you're here and she's not leaving until she sees you."

I was at a loss. It couldn't be Tamara; she knew exactly where I was.

Lola?

Would she be so brazen as to confront me?

Or maybe it was Skip. Maybe he'd paid Caleb to suggest it was a woman.

"I'll be right over," I said.

I explained the situation to Finn – to the extent I understood it, at least.

"I'll come with you."

We dressed hastily and, looking at the sky, took my car.

"Storm coming," Finn said. "It's supposed to get ugly later."

He was right; the wind was picking up, and it felt as though a storm was coming, though sooner rather than later. Leaves swirled in the air. We pulled up in front of Ocean Manor and entered the lobby. Caleb stopped us as we passed the front desk.

"This way," he said nervously.

Finn and I exchanged glances, but followed him as he led us to a private dining room.

Kitty Wolcott sat waiting at the head of the table.

Chapter **Eight**

I could feel Finn react viscerally at my side and knew though I'd described her appropriately, there was nothing quite like seeing Kitty in person. There she sat, tall and frighteningly thin, a bright pink blazer with navy piping draped over her wide, sharp shoulders. Her hands were folded on the table before her, the yellowed nails of her right hand drumming lightly on the surface.

"I'll just leave you two?" Finn said uneasily, his eyebrows raised to me in query.

Kitty answered before I could.

"Oh no," she said. "Please sit. Stay." (I waited for her to say, "Good boy" as Finn took the seat across from her.) "You are Phinneas M. Berwick, III, correct?"

Now I sat, my eyes narrowing on Kitty as I wondered what the hell her game was today.

"Yes," he said. "And you are?"

"Kathryn Wolcott," Kitty said, the moles on her upper lip bobbing. I could tell Finn was having trouble maintaining eye contact. Those damn moles got everyone. "Widow of Dr. Henry

Wolcott - you've heard of him, I'm sure?" She paused, but Finn said nothing. "And my son, Skip, is married to your...*friend* here, Eve."

"Kitty," I cut in impatiently. "What is this about?"

She said nothing, just let the smallest, most bemused little smile cross her lips. I suddenly understood what the proverbial cat who swallowed the canary must have looked like.

"Finn," I said, placing my hand lightly on his forearm. "Just go. I'll call you when I'm done here."

Kitty chuckled.

"Oh no, *Finn*," she purred. "Really. Stay. I feel like I know you already, and I'm sure you'll be interested in this conversation."

She reached into the massive Coach handbag perched on the chair beside her and produced a large manila envelope. Suddenly I knew. It was like every film noir, that moment when the private eye produces the incriminating photos. She set the envelope on the table between us, and I reached for it. I opened it. I couldn't help myself.

Finn exhaled miserably, pinching his temples between his thumb and forefinger. I thumbed through the sheaf of 8x10 glossy images, all slightly grainy and taken from an obvious distance, but each more graphic than the one before.

"Those are just my favorites, of course," Kitty said. "The full file is digital, and much too large to print out. It's amazing the way technology works these days. The number of pictures that camera can take in a matter of seconds! It's like watching a film. What do they call that? Stop-motion animation?"

176

Indeed. Stop-motion animation of Finn going down on me. Of me going down on Finn. Of that remarkable thing he did from behind. And now here I was, reliving the moments with Kitty sitting smugly across from me.

I shoved the pictures back into the envelope.

"Okay, Kitty, you win," I said. "I've been bad. I wish I had pictures of your son and the nanny - or of your son and any of the countless other women he's fucked during the course of our marriage - but I guess I was neglectful of those Kodak moments. Once again, you are so much more on the ball than I am. What's my punishment this time?"

"Well now, there's so much more to discuss here than punishment," Kitty began. "You've brought a third party into your marriage, haven't you? And there are the children to think of ..."

"*My* children," I bristled, "and I am always thinking of them. Don't drag them into this."

Kitty put a hand to her chest, presumably over the location where her heart should have been.

"Those boys are my grandsons, and I wouldn't drag them into anything hurtful for the world. Let's keep the blame where it belongs, shall we? Have another peek inside that folder, Eve." She let out a *tsk-tsk* sound. "*Always* thinking of them," she mocked. "I would certainly hope you weren't thinking of your children while you had a mouthful of Mr. Berwick here."

"That's enough," Finn said, standing. "Come on, Eve. You don't have to listen to this. Not from the woman who raised the philandering asshole you married."

Kitty clapped as if delighted.

"Oooh! Sticks and stones!" She hardened her gaze and lowered her voice. "Though you might want to be careful about raising questions of character, Mr. Berwick. And you're going to want to sit back down."

A feeling of apprehension came over me as Finn again took his seat, though I wasn't sure why. Hadn't the worst already happened?

"Now where were we?" Kitty mused, clearly enjoying her charade. "Oh, yes. My grandsons. I do worry about the sort of people they are exposed to, especially now that I know that you, Eve, are leading a rather tawdry double life."

I bit my tongue. I allowed myself one small Ally McBeal-esque moment to keep my growing dread at bay: a clear visual of myself leaping over the table and gouging Kitty's eyeballs from their dry, wrinkled sockets.

"Get to the fucking point, Kitty," I hissed.

"Language!" She scolded, shaking her head. "Eve, darling, I am just a concerned grandmother. How well do you know Mr. Berwick here? I mean, aside from the biblical sense." She chuckled at her own little joke. "Do you know, for example, that he has a daughter?"

Caught off guard, I gave Kitty the satisfaction she sought. My head whipped around to face Finn, whose stricken expression betrayed the truth.

"Ah, no, I gather not," Kitty said, her voice practically humming with pleasure. "Then I suppose you also don't know that he's failed to support the child. All that money of his, and she's not received a single penny. What do they call that? 'Deadbeat dad,' is it?"

For a moment I forgot about Kitty and my determination to maintain my composure. I turned slowly to Finn.

"You said you had no kids," I whispered.

"I can explain, but not here," he said, his eyes still cast down. "Not in front of her."

"It's true, then? Jesus, what's her name? How old is she?"

"Her name is Molly, and she's fifteen," Kitty chimed in.

"Oh, shut the fuck up already," I raged, standing and leaning across the table so my nose was mere inches from Kitty's mole-encrusted face. For the first time, she looked taken aback. "You've done enough damage. Go on home and have your goddamned Cosmopolitan and gloat."

I backed off and Kitty smoothed her blouse as though I'd physically roughed her up. She stood, picked up her bag, and then motioned as if having a last-minute thought.

"Just one more thing," she said.

"Eve Wolcott?"

At the sound of the unfamiliar male voice, I turned. A middle-aged man in khakis and a golf shirt stood there. It wasn't until I saw the Sheriff's badge suspended on the lanyard around his neck that I understood.

"You're Eve Wolcott of 232 Peaceful Lane in Jamestown?" he asked.

"Yes."

He placed a thick bundle of papers into my hands.

"You've been served," he said.

Kitty pranced from the room without a backward glance. I was left standing there with Finn, with the discomfort and questions that hung between us, and with the papers that informed me that Skip had filed for divorce.

What I wanted to do was be alone.

I wanted to curl up in a little ball on my hotel bed and wait for housekeeping to come wrap me up inside the sheets, send me down the chute, bleach and boil and launder and iron me until I was new and fresh.

I wanted to disappear.

I wanted to find a surgeon skillful enough to cut this lump from my throat, extract it neatly with all the sadness and hurt still attached, then sew me up so I could heal seamlessly around the hollow space left behind.

But I also wanted Finn to explain about his daughter, the one he'd said didn't exist. I wanted him to explain this giant lie so I could catalogue and file it, shelve it alongside the myriad lies I'd heard over the years from Skip. I wanted to pick it apart - to pick him apart - and try to understand. Were all men liars? And what, then, about women? Could we only defend ourselves by becoming liars, too? Is that what I'd done? Attempted to shield myself from pain by leaping from the bed of one liar into the bed of another, only to become a liar myself in the process?

And look how that had worked.

Not even six full days had passed since I arrived at Ocean Manor. Less than a week. A blip in the course of a lifetime. And yet that blip seemed to be the axis on which my entire life had turned. After so many years of enduring Skip's infidelities, I'd chosen one as the final straw. I'd used it to liberate myself from my marriage vows. I'd made it my excuse for pretending I was someone I wasn't, someone without obligations and responsibilities. I'd made my bed with Skip long ago, yet I'd gone rolling around in the sand with Finn. All the laughter and adventure and flirting and sex had been holding back this: the tsunami of grief that would wash me away at any second.

I walked down to the beach with Finn trailing at my heels, a recalcitrant child who knows he must explain his misbehavior but dreads it all the same. A wind had picked up from the north, stirring the water into a froth of whitecaps and chilling the air enough that the beach was nearly empty. The cabanas rippled with the strength of the breeze, and two young men wrested beach umbrellas closed. I watched a woman pull sweatshirts over the heads of her two small children and pack their sand toys into an orange-striped canvas bag. She herded them onto the path to the hotel as we passed.

I found a spot at the edge of the water, where the sand met the jetty, and seated myself on one of the massive slabs of granite. Cold seeped from the rock into my bones. I wrapped my thin sweater around me, crossing my arms and tucking the fabric against the wind. Finn moved to take his rumpled plaid shirt off and wrap it around me, but I shrugged him away. I wanted to be cold.

He sat in silence beside me for several minutes.

"What do you want to know?" he asked at last.

"All of it."

He hesitated so long before responding that I almost wondered if he'd heard me, or if my voice had been too small, too quiet. It seemed possible. I felt so slight and insignificant.

"I was married," he began.

I resisted the inappropriate urge to laugh. Mr. No Commitment. Married? Go figure.

"Her name was Dani, and I knew I'd fallen in love with her when I couldn't pass the coffee shop where she worked without stopping in. I don't drink coffee. Anyway, it didn't last long," he continued. "Not even a year. This was well before I made my money. It was before I made any money at all. We both worked and could never seem to pay the bills. And she was...not well. Bipolar. We fought all the time.

"I came home one day, thinking she was working late, but she never came back. Just walked away. I wasn't sure at first if she'd left me or if something awful had happened to her. She was always risk-taking when she was in a manic phase. Drinking and partying. It was days before the police would even take a missing-persons report, and their only angle seemed to be that I'd done something to her. It's always the husband, right? Basically, no one but me actually looked for her, and it

182

wasn't easy. This was almost sixteen years ago. I had no cell phone, no internet. She had no family or even friends, really. Just the people she'd party with, and none of them knew anything when the police came calling. She just vanished.

"Fast-forward about six years, and I'm finally making money – more than I could have imagined. I'm still legally married to a woman I haven't seen since that day she left for work and didn't come home, only now I have the resources to find her. I hire a private investigator and he tracks her down.

"Turns out she's gotten her life together. She's living in Ohio, married for about two years at that point. To a psychiatrist, appropriately enough. She has a baby boy, and she has a daughter, Molly. Six years old and a dead ringer for yours truly."

I listened to Finn, trying to imagine what it would be like to find out you were a father six years after the child had been born. I didn't look at him. I was still waiting for the rest of the story.

"I didn't tell Dani I knew about her daughter when I called, or that I suspected she was mine, too. I just told her I wanted to talk. That she could sign the divorce papers so I could move on, and that would be that. I flew out to Ohio and met her." He chuckled sadly. "In a coffee shop, of course."

He paused, and I couldn't help but look at him. This was a side of Finn I hadn't seen before, this solemn man on the verge of tears. This, I cautioned myself, was how the liars sucked you in. Fairly or not, I was reminded of Skip's tears over his father's death, the way our similar losses had made me feel bound to him. Men in tears were dangerous in my world.

"She was a different person. I wouldn't have believed it if I hadn't seen it myself. She was happy, genuinely happy. But when I showed her the picture the private investigator had given me, the one of Molly, she crumbled. See, I was dead, apparently. That was the story Molly had been told all her life, and it was the same story Dani told her new husband.

"I was furious. I'd had no choice. Dani had gone and made these big, crazy decisions all on her own."

"Why?" I asked.

I couldn't help but wonder at the other side of the story. There was always another side to the story.

Finn drew a deep breath.

"Dani said she knew if she told me she was pregnant, I would want her to have an abortion."

"And would that have been true?" I asked after a beat.

Finn pursed his lips, exhaling loudly through his nose.

"Maybe," he said. "Maybe not. How do I know? I wasn't given the choice, was I?"

I said nothing, just watched as he curled and uncurled his fists.

"She was probably right," he admitted at last. "I wouldn't have wanted a baby. I mean, Dani was frigging *nuts*, and we were broke and fighting constantly, and I just wasn't ready for kids. I wasn't sure if I ever would be. And yeah, I'm sure she knew all of this, so she ran away.

"I stormed out of that meeting with her, but she came to my hotel there in Ohio. One of those godawful places by the airport, you know, where you could be anywhere in the world and it's all the same. I just remember the sound of the planes overhead while she begged me not to ruin her life. 'If not for me, do it for Molly,' she said, and what the hell could I do? How do you tell a six year old kid that the father she's always been told is dead is actually alive? And oh yeah, the mother she's always trusted is a pathological liar? How royally would that screw a little kid up? I mean, even I could understand that.

"Dani said she'd sign the divorce papers if I'd go away and never contact her again. I told her I could pay child support - as much as she'd ever need and then some - but she was afraid the money would lead her husband to find out about me. So she signed the divorce papers and I left. I had my lawyers and my finance guy set up some accounts for Molly. If Dani ever changes her mind, the money's waiting for her."

"And if not?" I asked, barely able to speak.

Finn shrugged.

"Then when I die, Molly will become that person we all dream of being: the one with the rich uncle she never knew about who dies and leaves his millions to her."

I sat in stunned silence.

Finn shifted, reaching into his pocket. From his wallet, he pulled out a small cache of laminated photos and handed them to me. I flipped through them, watching a small, dark-haired girl with large, bright eyes grow into a stunning young woman. She looked so much like Finn it was heartbreaking. I flipped back and forth through them, wondering at the jumble of feelings this girl and her story inspired. At last I cupped them in my palms, my thumbs trapping them there as the wind whipped around us.

"How did you get these?" I asked.

"Dani sends them. I get a package in the mail every year. Photos and school papers and report cards. She's beautiful, isn't she?"

I handed the photos back to him, my eyes tearing up. I stood as Finn folded the pictures back into his wallet.

"I think," I began, struggling not to cry. "I think that's the saddest thing ever."

I started off down the beach, but Finn followed. He caught my arm and turned me to face him.

"Eve," he said. The plea in his voice made my name sound like a prayer, the desperate kind drowning men make.

I whirled at him.

"You are a sad, selfish man," I cried, the tears finally streaming down my face. "That poor girl! You'll dump all your money on her when you're gone, but god forbid you do a damn thing for her while you're here. No, you'll sit around, with her pictures and report cards and tell yourself you're a good person, then off you go to paraglide and surf and fuck around with whomever the hell you want. You're not a father, you're a selfish jerk. You may fool yourself, Skip, but you don't fool me."

I heard my slip, too damn Freudian to stand, and didn't even care. I tore up the path toward the hotel.

"Eve!" Finn called after me.

But he didn't follow, and in no time at all, the sound of his voice was lost on the wind.

186

Chapter **Nine**

I looked at the date as I passed the front desk. That couldn't be right, could it? But it was, right there in black and white. Less than a week had passed since I'd arrived at Ocean Manor. It felt like a year. Longer, even.

I tipped the valet and climbed behind the wheel of my car, this time with the top up. It was windy and there was a chill in the air, and besides, having the top down felt too carefree for my mood. I turned left onto the road, though turning right would have been the more direct route. I didn't want to drive past Finn's house.

I made the drive to Stonington in silence, with a lump in my throat. I'd spent the previous two hours on the phone, trying to make some semblance of order out of my suddenly-messy life. I'd tried to reach Skip, in vain once again. I'd gotten Eli on the phone and confirmed that neither he nor Max had spoken with their father or their grandmother recently. I'd spoken with one of the divorce attorneys Wally had recommended, a James Kingsley, III, and had transferred a retainer to his bank. He, in turn, was taking steps to be sure neither Skip nor Kitty pulled the boys from Morefield. I didn't think they would (they were all about that damn school), but this, I was told, was the way things were done. Standard operating procedure.

"Can *I* pull the boys from school?" I asked.

I wanted to drive straight to Morefield, bring them home, bake cookies and play board games. Play pretend. Postpone the inevitable.

But James Kingsley, III, whom I'd never met, told me I needed to leave my children at boarding school. He said something about parental fitness, stability, and even kidnapping. My head spun. He promised he would arrange for Skip and me to meet with the boys together, to share the burden of telling them their family had come apart at the seams.

After all that, I'd called Wally and given him the update, then called Tamara and cried freely.

"Get your skinny little ass down here," she'd said. "Nate and Ian will gladly share the guest cottage, and we need you here for Nana's service."

I'd hesitated.

"I should go home, try to talk to Skip. I've got to make sure he doesn't talk to the boys alone. God knows, he's not known for tact or empathy."

"True," Tamara said. "But wait and see what your lawyer has to say when he talks to Skip's lawyer. Stay with us tonight, we'll have the service in the morning, and by then maybe someone will have spoken to Skip and you can make a plan."

This is what my life has come to, I thought as I neared Tamara's house. *I'm having my lawyer call Skip's lawyer.*

As a last-ditch effort, I punched the Bluetooth button and gave Skip's cell one more try.

"Skip, please," I said to his voice mailbox. "Just call me. We have to make a plan for telling the boys. They're at such a tough age. Please. Call me. Okay?"

I hung up, realizing I sounded as deflated as I felt. The anger over Lola and the fun of letting all hell break loose with Finn were a distant memory. I thought of calling my doctor, asking for a refill of my full-strength meds. Maybe now wasn't the best time to try reality without my little helpers. Maybe when reality was this sucky, drugs were a good idea.

"No," I said aloud, as if verbally rebutting the idea was the only way to get past it. "You're on the right path. Just hang in there."

Great. Now I was talking to myself.

I made the turn into the long drive that led to Tamara and Howard's house, passing the split-rail gate that always stood open. The driveway was lined with evenly-spaced oaks so old they'd been stately already when Nana was born. The property had been a working farm then, and Nana's mother had given birth to fourteen babies right in the main house. Only six had lived to adulthood. Five had left Connecticut as soon as they were able, but Nana stayed. She took over the farm and raised her only child - Tamara's mother, Debra - in the same house. It was something of a local scandal, as Nana never married and never named Debra's father, but rumor had it he was as married as Nana was not.

Over time, the farm was partitioned and parcels sold off just to pay the taxes. The fields and barn were rented out, and an indoor riding ring was constructed to keep the property self-supporting. Debra married Glen, the contractor who'd built the riding ring, and they'd raised Tamara and her brother Nate there in the farmhouse. Nana moved into the guest house (a former chicken coop), and there she stayed, the one constant as everything around her changed. Debra and Glen retired, buying a condo in Florida and spending half the year there. Tamara married Howard, bought the farmhouse from her parents, and started having babies.

The property still looked much as it had the first time I'd seen it, back in late September of my first year at Mount Holyoke. Tamara had been feeling homesick, so we'd driven to Stonington for the weekend. Then as now, the first signs of autumn were evident: leaves just beginning to turn and fall, the grass at the edges of the long gravel drive beginning to yellow, the smell of wood smoke in the air. I remembered pulling my sad little Toyota up in front of the rambling old house, seeing Tamara's brother Nate (a junior in high school at the time) come barreling through the front door like a golden retriever, his parents and Nana close behind. I remembered feeling a split-second pang of sadness, thinking of my mother at home alone. My only family. I knew in an instant that I wanted to belong to a family like Tamara's, loud and loving, and they warmly welcomed me in.

Today I had to bring my car to a stop well before I

reached the front porch, as a wild tangle of little boys was wrestling on the front lawn.

"Auntie Eve's here!" I heard one of them cry from somewhere in the midst of the madness, and then they began to peel off from one another, racing toward me as I climbed from the driver's seat and braced myself.

"Take it easy, hooligans," Nate called, stepping out onto the porch with a smile.

I smiled back, even let out a little laugh as Nate caught Reed and Warhol, scooping them up and effortlessly carrying them as they wriggled in his arms. I found myself in a crush of boyish movement as Nate hugged me and the kids scrambled to see if I'd brought treats. I usually brought candy. As if the little devils needed sugar, right? But Tam and Howard were so strict with the organic/whole/vegetarian diet they fed their boys, I kind of felt badly for them. What was childhood without a candy necklace now and then? Plus, candy scored me major auntie points. Points I would not be getting today.

"Sorry," I said, holding out my empty palms.

"Bad auntie!" Wynn cried.

He hauled off and kicked me in the shins with his pint-sized little feet. Turns out even pint-sized little feet can hurt like hell. I drew in a sharp breath of air and tried not to double over. Wynn took off running.

"Wynn, is that how we say hello to auntie?" Tamara called, apparently having appeared on the porch just in time to witness the assault.

Wynn stuck his tongue out at her and ran off toward the

tire swing.

"Sorry, babe," Tamara said, giving me a hug as Nate shooed the other boys away.

She kept her arm around me as we walked up the front steps. Ian, Debra and Glen all waited on the porch and took turns hugging me.

"Hey, Eve," Ian said, his usual monotone a degree more somber.

"Oh, Eve, it's just too awful," Debra cried.

She was a frazzled faux blonde who always seemed on the verge of tears over the latest perceived tragedy. I wasn't sure if, this time, the tragedy was the loss of Nana at age ninety-eight or the demise of my marriage.

"She was so vibrant!" Debra went on. "She really should have had so many good years still ahead of her!"

Nana.

Glen rolled his eyes and disappeared into the house. He was so good at disappearing when Debra got going, he could have been a magician.

"All right, Mom, enough," Tamara said firmly, shooting Debra a glance.

And then Howard made his entrance. Howard always made an entrance.

He stepped through the front door and onto the porch as if following stage directions. He wore artfully torn and paint-splattered jeans, a navy button-down shirt I'd have bet was Paul Jones, an assortment of rings and earrings, and a fedora. He'd grown a goatee since I'd last seen him. He looked like Johnny

Depp in his pirate incarnation, but with less eyeliner.

"Eve, sweetheart," he purred.

I caught sight of Nate as he passed behind Howard. He was pointing at Howard, then himself, then raising his eyebrows and shrugging. It was his longstanding joke where Howard and his flamboyance was concerned: *Okay, who's the resident gay guy here?* I could hear the words as clearly as if Nate had said them, and I had to stifle a laugh.

"Howard," I said.

He took my hands in his and then kissed them, first one, then the other. Even Tamara was rolling her eyes now. He leaned in close, as if to share a confidence, but with Howard, every word was always spoken loudly enough for an audience to hear.

"That Skip," he seethed. "Biggest. Loser. Ever. If you were my wife, I'd treasure you."

"All right, all right," Tamara said. "I'll leave you the key to the guest house if you want to continue the sap-fest later. For now? Dinner."

Howard put on his best wounded face, then turned and went back into the house.

"I'd say he almost *sashayed*," Nate murmured to me as we followed. "Very Zoolander."

I bit my tongue and punched his arm.

Dinner was the event it always was at Tamara and Howard's. The food - all organic and vegetarian - was elaborate and delicious. Tamara might have liked to claim responsibility, but it was the work of Meri, the nutritionist and chef who did their shopping and prepared their meals in exchange for free board for her horse. There was quinoa with cilantro and lime, an amazing roast eggplant and tomato dish, vegan cheese with a rich cashew flavor, and thick slices of the homemade bread that Ian enjoyed making almost as much as I enjoyed eating it. The wine flowed endlessly, the conversation equally so. The kids came and went from the dinner table, occasionally climbing up onto a corner of the long farmhouse table while Tam and Howard gently requested that they not do so. I felt slightly out of it, too disconnected from my own life to enjoy myself as I usually did.

"Wait," Nate said, and I realized I hadn't been paying attention to the conversation at all. "Remember when Eli was born? And Nana put Miss Kitty in her place?"

Across the table, poor Ian looked lost. He and Nate had been together nearly six years, but that still wasn't long enough for him to be privy to half the topics of conversation that surfaced at family dinner parties. I gave him a sympathetic smile.

"Yes!" Tamara cried excitedly, laughing so hard she snorted. "Remember, Eve? You were living in that rented house on the East Side, and you'd literally just come in the door from the hospital..." She lowered her voice. "After all you'd just been through," she hissed, and I knew she meant Skip's antics more than childbirth.

"And in comes Miss Kitty, dressed to the nines," Nate continued. *"Where's that grandson of mine?"* he mimicked.

"And she goes poking one of those long finger nails of

hers into poor Eli's little face," Tamara said, making her index finger into a claw. "And then *bam!* Nana is *in her face,* telling her how nails that long are unhygienic, and she shouldn't be poking them anywhere near a new baby."

Nate and Howard collapsed in laugher.

"I thought she'd die," Howard said. "That anyone would *dare* suggest to Kitty Wolcott that there was anything unhygienic about her…"

"I mean, that woman's asshole is probably devoid of bacteria," Tamara said.

"I don't think she has an asshole," Nate said sweetly.

"Probably why she's so full of shit," Howard added.

I laughed in spite of myself.

Later, after the dishes had been cleared and Howard herded the kids upstairs for bedtime, Tamara walked with me to the guest cottage.

"Nate and Ian already took over Nana's bedroom," she said. "I hope you're okay with the sofa?"

"Absolutely," I said.

"You were awfully quiet tonight."

"Sorry."

"It wasn't a criticism," Tamara clarified.

She pulled me into a hug. Tears sprang to my eyes.

"Fucking talk to me," Tam said at last, pressing her nose to mine.

I laughed through my tears. I sat down on the sofa in Nana's cottage while Tamara wandered into the kitchen. She returned with two solid glasses and a bottle of scotch. She poured while I searched for – and found – a box of Kleenex.

"Okay, first things first," Tamara said, handing me a glass. "What? The? Fuck? All the bullshit Skip puts you through, like, *forever*, and he fucking files for divorce first? On what grounds?"

"Adultery and abandonment," I said, rolling my eyes at the irony.

"What the fuck is up with that?" Tamara gasped.

I took a sip of the scotch.

"Kitty is what the fuck is up with that," I said simply. "I can't even get Skip on the phone."

"And he loves his phone," Tamara acknowledged.

I nodded.

"Primarily because he's sexting with who-knows-whom," I specified.

"Bitch probably took it from him," Tam laughed. "Kitty's probably got him locked away in a turret in that ridiculous fucking house of hers. Like goddamned Rapunzel."

I laughed loudly.

"Receding-hairline Rapunzel!" I contributed.

The scotch was already doing wonderful things to my brain. I could picture Skip trying to let down his curls, could see Lola trying to climb up them.

"And what about fuckbuddy Finn?" Tamara asked, forcing me to sharply shift gears.

I took another sip, squeezing my eyes shut. God, how I'd been trying not to think about Finn. My stomach bottomed out at the mere mention of his name.

"Finn is not what he seemed," I said, then reconsidered. "Or maybe he is exactly what he seemed. He is a noncommittal asshole."

"You said that on the phone earlier," Tamara said, "but I'm still not getting the whole picture."

"He's a deadbeat dad," I said decisively. "He told me he had no kids, but he's got a teenage daughter he hasn't ever even met. And all that money of his? The poor kid hasn't seen a penny."

Tamara sat in stunned silence, a rare state for her.

"There has to be more to the story," she said at last.

I wrinkled my nose at her.

"There is," I conceded, "but I'm not sure it redeems him any."

Tamara was silent a few moments more. She swirled the remaining scotch in her glass, then downed it.

"Listen," she said. "Here's what I think. You've been through nearly two decades of bullshit with Skip. You juggle like a fucking circus clown, and I'm sure all your 'friends' from the ladies guild think you're the shit. But I know you. You've been a sad-sack, pill-popping zombie for far too long."

"Thanks for the pep talk," I muttered sarcastically, but Tamara kept going.

"No – listen. The other day? What I stumbled onto in our suite at Ocean Manor wasn't just a hungover housewife with an alarming, naked-mole-rat-pussy. Hell, no! You were The Red Fox again. You were on your game and shining like the fucking northern star. You know, aside from the whole dry-heaving-over-the-toilet business. I mean, *shit*, you had Adam Levine bringing you doughnuts!"

"I still don't know who that is..." I interjected.

"Doesn't matter," Tamara said, shaking her head. "Whether it was Finn or you or some combination of the two of you, you were a hot shit. None of that mousy-deferential crap that flies at the yacht club. You were *you*, only better. You were determined. Do you know what I mean?"

I did. But I didn't say so. I looked into my glass, brought it to my lips for a final swig.

"Evie, I love you," Tamara said, sliding closer to me and putting her hands on my shoulders. "I'm not saying this Finn guy is the answer to your troubles, or that you should even give him another chance. I'm not in your shoes and I don't know the whole story. I'm just saying that whatever went on while you were with him, it did something good for you. I'm glad it happened, and it fucking sucks that Skip beat you to the punch on the divorce, but just hang in there and the end result will be the same. You'll move on, and you'll be awesome."

I said it out loud, then, the thing that frightened me most. It just came out of me, impulsively.

"What if he gets the kids? What if he takes Max and Eli away from me?"

I lost it, collapsing in tears. I reached blindly for the Kleenex.

Tamara gathered me into her arms.

"Are you fucking kidding? Skip couldn't keep a gerbil alive. The courts will see that in a nanosecond." She pulled

198

back, her hands gripping my shoulders, and looked keenly into my face. "And you know what? It wouldn't matter anyway. They're too old to be pawns in a game. Those boys love you. Eli's your mini-me, and Max? He may be Skip's little clone, but sooner or later that'll work in your favor, too. Skip's a mama's boy if I've ever seen one."

I laughed through my tears, sending snot flying onto Tamara's arm. She wiped it away easily.

"Ah, yeah, no wonder sweet-ass Finn went for you," she joked. "You're a fucking hottie."

"Thank you, Tam," I said.

She tipped her head, dismissing me gently. She cleared our glasses, then pulled some blankets and a pillow from a cupboard and set them on the edge of the sofa. Then she turned and I walked her to the door.

"You'll get through this," she told me. "And you'll be better for it in the long run, truly. You and the boys, both."

I nodded.

"I'll get up early and help you get ready for the service," I promised.

"Shouldn't take much. It's just us. All Nana's friends were already dead."

"I guess that's the trouble with living to ninety-eight," I allowed.

"We'll set a few chairs down by the pond, say the things we should, and scatter her ashes there. She loved it there."

"Sounds perfect," I said.

Tamara left, and I settled into the sofa with the blankets

and pillows she'd given me. It was strange; aside from Nate and Ian's belongings scattered here and there, the cottage looked just as it always had when Nana lived there, yet somehow it was clear she was gone. I felt the damned familiar lump return to my throat, and I swallowed.

I plugged my phone in to charge and checked to see if I had any messages.

There was nothing.

My finger scrolled, pulled up the last of the texts I'd received from Finn. So light, so playful. So wrong.

So why did I feel as I did when I thought of him? Sad or lost or whatever the hell this was?

"Forget him," I told myself.

I texted Max and Eli a quick "xo," hoping that wasn't too helicopter-parent-ish.

I heard Nate and Ian approaching the cottage and I closed my eyes, feigning sleep so I wouldn't have to make small talk.

And then I lay there, listening to them brush their teeth and change out of their clothes, settle into bed with books or iPads, exchange a few whispers and a goodnight kiss. The mundane movements of a marriage. I fell asleep wondering if I would ever take such simple comforts for granted again.

I woke at dawn and walked down to the pond. Tamara, however, had clearly been up even earlier than me.

The white Adirondack chairs that usually sat here and there around the pond had been gathered together in the shade on one bank. Draped over the back of each one was one of the many quilts Nana had made in her lifetime, each commemorating a birth, a marriage, a goal achieved. A fluttering noise caught my attention, and I saw that the branches of the weeping willow above appeared to be full of tiny, white birds. Walking closer, I saw that they were not birds, but paper snowflakes. There had to be several dozen of them, all suspended from the tree on thin bits of twine and making a light, lovely sound in the breeze.

"The boys made them," Tamara said, walking up behind me.

"They're beautiful," I said.

"They didn't even try to stab each other with the scissors," Tamara added with a note of maternal pride.

I smiled.

"I know it's not the right season, but Nana loved a good snow storm."

A tear slipped down Tamara's cheek, and I pulled her into a hug.

An hour later we were all gathered at the water's edge. Tamara read one of Nana's favorite poems by Edna St. Vincent Millay. Nate told a story about how he'd gotten in trouble in kindergarten for allegedly kissing a girl. "Nana knew I'd done no such thing," he said, and we all laughed. Ian gazed at Nate with such love I felt warmed by it. Debra kept her tears and melodrama to a minimum, and Glen sat in grateful silence beside her. Howard sat stoically behind round-rimmed sunglasses, but I saw him dab at his eyes with a paisley handkerchief. Even the boys seemed subdued.

"I gave them tea with Valerian," Tamara whispered to me, and I clapped a hand to my mouth to stifle my laughter.

For Tamara, giving her kids tea with a natural sleep aid was akin to doping them up. And it was a wise move.

My thumb and forefinger played with the edge of the quilt on my chair. Somewhere, I had the quilt Nana had made when I'd graduated Mount Holyoke. It had been on my bed for years, then was tucked away when I became more concerned with decor than sentiment. I would have to find it.

Ian stood and joined Nate at the edge of the pond. We all followed. Tamara helped Nate open the urn, and they scattered Nana's ashes into the breeze.

"That was perfect," I told Tamara as she took my hand. "Nana would have loved that."

"I think so," she agreed.

The boys had sensed it was safe to misbehave again, and they were tearing across the lawn toward the house.

"Meri's working on quite a brunch," Tamara said.

"Nice. I'll be up in a minute. Want to check my phone," I explained.

I retreated to the guest cottage, hoping for a text from the boys. It was probably still too early to hear back from the lawyer, and I didn't let myself think too much about whether or not I might hear from Finn.

I swiped the screen and my heart lurched.

I'd missed eight phone calls, all from unfamiliar numbers in Massachusetts.

Max and Eli were in Massachusetts.

Fearing the worst – a sailing accident, a head injury during lacrosse practice, a suicide attempt proving Eli was truly depressed and shouldn't have been left there – I checked my voice mail.

I listened to the message once, then again and again.

It couldn't be.

I listened again.

It couldn't be, but it was.

Skip was dead.

Chapter **Ten**

The next few days passed in an incomprehensible whirl of activity and grief. I learned that Skip had died at Lola's apartment in Boston, and an autopsy was ordered because of his age and the "surrounding circumstances." That turned out to be code for having-a-heart-attack-while-taking-Viagra-and-fucking-a-woman-half-his-age-and-not-his-wife.

Unlike Nana, Skip had made no funeral arrangements. He'd thought he had plenty of time, of course, so I was left with the task. I picked up the boys from Morefield and brought them home to Jamestown. Tamara came and stayed with us.

This is Skip's funeral.

That sentence ran through my head endlessly through the ordeal, but no matter how I tried to hammer the truth into my brain, it didn't take. Skip couldn't be dead. He just couldn't. He was *Skip*, for chrissakes. It had taken me long enough to adjust to the idea of becoming a divorcee. How could I be a widow?

Too many people in somber dress crowded into our home in Jamestown, filling the house where Eli and Max had learned to walk, to read, to use the potty. The air was humid and cloying. There were floral arrangements more stiff and formal than the roses Skip used to send me, and catered food set out by uniformed staff I didn't recall hiring. There were my boys, slight facsimiles of men, uncomfortably pulling at their collars and ties.

"Can I leave yet?" I asked Tamara.

"Sweetheart, you can do whatever the hell you want," she said gently. "Go lie down. I'll make your excuses."

But I didn't want to lie down. I didn't want to be alone with my thoughts.

"I'm okay," I lied. "I should stay here for the boys."

I looked at them again, and Eli caught me. He fanned his fingers in a halfhearted greeting. Beside him, Max slumped in his chair, picking at his shoelaces. I crossed the room and sat down between them.

"Hey. How are you guys doing?"

Eli shrugged.

"Okay," he said.

Max shot him a steely glance, then turned the evil eye on me.

"How do you think we're doing?" he spat, then he lowered his voice and mumbled, "Dumbass."

"Hey," I said, trying to be gentle but firm. "There's no need to talk like that."

"Like hell there isn't," Max said, digging his thumbnail

into the sole of his shoe and sounding alarmingly like Skip in a bad mood. When he raised his eyes, I saw that his anger had only intensified. "This is all your fault, you dumb cunt."

You could have knocked me over with a feather.

Max kicked his chair into the wall and pushed past me. A few people close to us turned and looked, but that was the least of my worries.

My twelve-year-old son had called me a cunt.

I don't think I'd ever even heard the word aloud before. I certainly had never used it. And worse than the word was Max's tone. Furious, dripping with disgust. Aiming to hurt. Aiming, and succeeding splendidly.

"I'm sorry," I said to Eli.

"What are you sorry for?" he asked. "He's the dick."

Great.

Now Eli was referring to his brother as a dick.

"I'm just sorry," I said truthfully. "I'd shield you and Max from any hurt, you know, but there's nothing I can do about this. Death is just...brutally unfair."

"I know," he said.

He reached out and cupped his hand over mine, the tips of his fingers squeezing my flesh reassuringly. The gesture was so adult, so kind, it threatened to unhinge me. I looked down at his hand and could picture those fingers when they were so small they could barely wrap around my pinkie, could recall those nails when they were tiny and translucent and I was afraid I'd hurt him by trimming them.

"I'll go talk to Max," I said, and then I stopped.

206

I looked up and I saw her, like a ghost at the door.

Lola.

How could she have come? How did she have that much nerve?

I went rigid as she spotted me eyeing her. I realized Eli had stiffened, too, and I glanced over at him. He knew, I realized then. Whether he'd seen or heard something that made him suspect, or had simply figured it out because he was so intuitive, Eli knew. He looked at me sideways, his shoulders straightening protectively.

"Mom?"

"It's okay, kidface," I said, grateful my voice sounded even though I felt anything but. "I've got this."

I stood and Lola bolted like a fawn. I pushed through the crowd and followed her through the front door and down the steps. Because even the weather had conspired to make the day miserable, it was raining.

"Wait!" I called, stopping Lola amidst the downpour and the crush of parked cars in the driveway.

She turned and froze, the rain soaking through her black dress and sending her eye makeup cascading down her cheeks.

"I'm sorry," she cried. "I don't know why I came. I just meant to watch from outside. The boys...I was thinking... I don't know what I was thinking."

I didn't know what she was thinking, either. Or what I was thinking, for that matter. I stepped closer.

"The coroner told me how he died," I said. "Cocaine and Viagra?"

"I told him that was stupid," she said, shaking her head. "He didn't need either one."

I laughed in spite of myself.

"No, I'm sure he didn't," I said.

While I had been worrying that Skip and Lola were shacked up in my house here in Jamestown, it turned out they'd been in her bed in her little apartment in Boston. I wondered if he'd thought at all about the irony of that, if he'd remembered our early days in my little Boston efficiency.

"I really am sorry," Lola said, sniffing. "I'm sure you hate me. You should."

"I don't hate you," I said reflexively, realizing only after the words were out that they were true.

"I hate me," she breathed. "I betrayed you."

I tried, then, to hate her. I really did. She *had* betrayed me. I'd let her into my home, entrusted her with my children, and what had she done? She'd fucked my husband. Fucked him to death, as it turned out. I should have hated her. But the truth was, I knew Skip, and all I saw in front of me now was a young woman who wouldn't have stood a chance against his charm.

"Please," she choked out, sobbing now. "I'm so sorry. I couldn't help myself. I love... I loved him."

I almost smiled then, because I knew how fully she believed that was true, and I also knew that she would look back on this moment in twenty years and wonder how she'd been so naïve.

"Just go," I said. "I believe you, and I'm not angry. I just can't deal with one more thing right now. Okay?"

She nodded, and I waited for her to leave, but she seemed rooted to the spot. So I turned, drenched by the rain that fell without mercy, and I made my way back to the warm glow of the lights spilling out onto the porch.

I made my way upstairs without acknowledging the guests who saw me pass. Two of the women from my book club, Rachel Moss and Jamie Wexler, looked as though they felt snubbed. I was beyond caring.

I went into my bathroom and peeled off my wet skirt and blouse, then changed into black leggings and a cotton tunic. Then I went to talk with Max.

I found him in his room, twirling and jabbing a lacrosse stick in the air like a weapon. That he was doing this inside the house was against the rules, but seemed significantly beside the point under the circumstances. My foot hit a floorboard that creaked, and he whipped around to face me, clutching the stick to his chest. His blonde curls fell over his eyes.

"We need to talk," I said.

"I'm sorry," he sighed exaggeratedly in a most un-sorry tone.

Max's knee-jerk reaction whenever he was in any kind of trouble was either to deny culpability (if he thought he could possibly get away with it), or to apologize instantly and try to head off any discussion of the subject. Again, just like Skip.

"That's not going to work this time," I explained.

I took the lacrosse stick from him and set it down by the door. Then I sat down on the edge of his bed.

"Listen," I said. "I know you're suffering right now, suffering horribly. We all are. What I don't understand is why you're angry with me. Dad's death was…an accident. He had a heart attack and just couldn't get to the hospital fast enough. Why would you think it was my fault?"

Max paced the room, kicking angrily at the fringe on the edges of the carpet and keeping his eyes focused on his feet.

"I'm not an idiot, you know. I heard Grandma on the phone," he said, then he turned his eyes to me accusingly. "You were going to divorce Dad. His heart attack wasn't an accident. He was upset over *you* and he took some kind of drugs or something, and he *died*. If it wasn't for you, he'd still be here!"

Goddamned Kitty. As if I needed one more reason to want to see her head on a platter.

"Oh, Max," I said. I reached for him and he batted my arms away. I chose my words carefully, fairly certain I was going to have to stretch the truth a bit. "You heard part of a conversation that wasn't accurate. Your dad and I had an argument, but that had *nothing* to do with his death. I loved your dad, very much, and the last thing I'd ever have wanted was for something like this to happen. If I could fix it, kiddo, and bring your dad back, I'd do it in a heartbeat, I promise."

And it was true. I was ready to move on to a life that

210

had less to do with Skip, but not this way. When Tamara and I had sung and danced around the hotel room at Ocean Manor, humorously imagining fifty ways to leave a husband, this wasn't on the list.

Max seemed to be winding down. I knew from experience that he would spend a good, long time alone in his room, probably playing one of the violent video games I'd never wanted in my house, but Skip had allowed. Maybe it served a purpose, though. Whenever Max emerged from his room after shooting things on the computer screen, he was much nicer to the rest of us.

But there was one more thing.

"Last issue," I said, a stern note to my voice. "That word."

Max's eyes flitted to my face, then away. He knew he was in deep.

"Where did you hear it?" I asked.

He shrugged.

"Dorm," he muttered. "Cameron Reis says it all the time."

Good old Morefield.

"I don't know if you understood what you were saying," I began, "but there are some words that are so brutal, so demeaning, you never say them. Ever. That is one of those words. Do you understand?"

Max nodded.

"I mean it. If that word ever comes out of your mouth again, I'm taking a page from my parents' playbook and you are eating a bar of soap for dinner. Got it?"

"Got it," Max said, chastised.

"I loved you before you were even born, I've loved you every day since, and I promise I will be your fiercest advocate all my days on earth," I said quietly. "That deserves some respect."

I wrapped him in a hug as I left the room, and planted a kiss on the top of his head. For once, he didn't resist.

I went in search of Kitty, planning to give her a piece of my mind about discussing Skip's death within earshot of the boys. I didn't have to look for long. The crowd had thinned to just a few people, and she moved determinedly among them, aiming for me. She was flanked by two men I didn't recognize at first, until they were taking my hand and offering their condolences. They were attorneys who'd handled the Wolcott family's matters for decades. I'd last seen them when signing my revised will shortly after Max's birth. The tall, thin man wearing wire-rimmed spectacles was Mark Fisher. The slightly shorter, thoroughly bald man was John Webb.

"We're so sorry to have to do this today," Fisher apologized, "but if you have a moment? If we could speak somewhere privately?"

"Is this about Skip's will?" I asked, confused.

It seemed highly unusual to be dealing with such a thing while the dining room table was still dotted with chicken salad rolls and relish trays for mourners.

Fisher and Webb exchanged a glance.

"Not exactly," Fisher said. "And I'm afraid it is somewhat urgent."

"Get in the study, then," Kitty said, shooing me and the attorneys in that direction.

"I'm afraid we have some bad news," Webb began when the door was closed.

I lowered myself into a seat at one side of the room, while Kitty found a chair in the opposite corner. Bad news was the last thing I needed more of.

"How much did each of you know about Skip's finances?" Fisher asked.

"I knew everything about Skip!" Kitty sniffed.

I shook my head. Truthfully, I'd left most, if not all, financial matters to Skip. I knew what the balance on the AmEx was, and how much money I had in my personal checking account. Other than that, it was all Skip.

"Did you know that he was bankrupt?" Webb said solemnly.

I felt as though I'd been slapped. Kitty recoiled, the color draining from her face.

"Nonsense!" she barked.

"Bankrupt? As in, no money?" I asked.

I thought suddenly and regretfully of my wedding and engagement rings, tossed into the surf in an ill-conceived moment of drunken determination. Talk about picking the wrong time to be bold.

Webb and Fisher nodded.

"That can't be," Kitty said. "What about his salary?"

Again, the dynamic duo exchanged a glance.

"You weren't aware of his work situation?" Fisher asked.

"What 'situation'?" I asked, afraid to hear the answer.

"Skip hadn't worked in two years. Not since he left the firm," Fisher explained.

"*Left the firm?*" Kitty and I cried in unison.

Webb and Fisher proceeded slowly from there. It seemed Skip's work performance had been declining, and there was some question of whether he might have been drinking too heavily or using drugs. He'd left the firm by mutual agreement two years ago, and never said anything to anyone. He'd continued going to Boston as if nothing had changed. Skip's finances went into a downward spiral parallel to his own. He'd drained our savings, stopped making payments on our life insurance policies, and the mortgage on our Jamestown home was currently two months past due. A month earlier, the Boston brownstone had been lost at foreclosure. Skip's Range Rover was scheduled to be repossessed, and my BMWs weren't far behind.

"We can save your home here," Webb stated, looking over paperwork before him. "If you, Mrs. Wolcott, will agree to a refinance of the mortgage."

I realized when he said 'Mrs. Wolcott,' he was looking at Kitty.

"I'm sorry," I said. "I don't understand. What does my mother-in-law have to do with the mortgage on my house?"

214

"The house is held in trust, correct?" Fisher asked.

"Yes," I said.

All our properties were held in trust. Eli and Max were beneficiaries.

Fisher peered through his glasses at the papers in front of him.

"She's the successor trustee," he said. "Yes, there it is. Kathryn Wolcott. Then you, of course, if she declines."

It couldn't be. Skip and I had discussed this, though it was a long time ago. He was the trustee, I was the successor, and Kitty was our back-up. I took the paperwork from Fisher and read through it. It all looked just as I recalled, with one glaring, crucial exception: Kathryn Wolcott was, indeed, named as the successor trustee.

In other words, Skip had left me with no money, and with control of our home – our only remaining asset – in Kitty's hands.

It was too much. I'd thought I'd hit rock bottom when I was served with divorce papers. Then Skip died, and it seemed things couldn't possibly get any worse. But now? Here I sat with Kitty, who remained sufficiently rocked by all we'd heard to require a drink, but who already looked heartened by news of the trusteeship. That was a gift, a return of some of the control she'd lost upon learning her beloved Skip hadn't been all she'd believed. I could already see the gears turning.

"Let me see if I understand this correctly?" she said at last, sipping her cocktail. "This house currently has a small mortgage and plenty of equity, correct? If I sign a mortgage, Eve

215

here will have the funds available to get back on her feet."

"That is correct," Webb confirmed.

"But if I don't, Eve has nothing, and the small mortgage will soon be foreclosed?"

"Unless Mrs. Wolcott has funds we are unaware of, that would seem to be the case, yes."

I saw where this was going, and as evil as I knew Kitty to be, I still couldn't believe it.

"Kitty," I said sharply. "Whatever our differences, surely you are not thinking of letting your grandsons end up homeless?"

Her eyes went wide and she clapped a hand to her chest (one of her favorite maneuvers). She made little clucking sounds with her mouth.

"What sort of heartless person do you think I am?" she asked, aghast.

I wanted desperately to reply.

I bit my lip.

"Certainly not," Kitty said. "Though I do think if I am going to be tasked with looking after this household, there should be some sort of formal agreement in place."

"There already is, Kitty," I said impatiently. "The trust."

"What about a guardianship?" she queried, turning to Fisher and Webb. "If I were given proper authority to oversee my grandsons' upbringing, I'd be happy to pay their tuition at Morefield – even beyond."

I shot out of my seat.

"Are you out of your mind?" I seethed. "You want me

216

to give you my children? What the hell is wrong with you?"

My anger failed to fluster Kitty. If anything, she seemed encouraged by it. The color had returned to her face. She drummed her long fingernails lightly on the arm of her chair.

"You'd still be their mother, of course," she said lightly. "But I would have some legal rights, as well. To make sure they're not exposed to unsavory company, for example. You may recall we've discussed this before? Also, to be sure they are properly educated. I was stunned to hear Eli say something about leaving Morefield for some art school – such a thought! If I could help you out of this nasty financial predicament, and help my grandsons in the process, doesn't that sound like a winning situation for everyone?"

Even Fisher and Webb appeared awestruck by this turn of events. Their heads turned from Kitty's face to mine and then back again, as if they were watching a tennis match. I waited until my anger had subsided enough for me to speak.

"Kitty," I said finally. "There are no winning situations here, and contrary to what you may believe, this isn't a game. Eli and Max are my children. One way or another, I will provide for them. I will decide – with their help – what they need and where to educate them. Now if you don't mind, I've just had the absolute shittiest day of my life, so I think it's time for you to slither on back to Newport and leave me and my children in peace."

I nodded at the attorneys.

"Gentlemen," i said curtly.

Then I left the library and made a beeline for Eli, Max and Tamara.

Chapter **Eleven**

"I hope you told her to go fuck herself," Tamara said.

The boys were asleep upstairs, and we were curled in chairs by the fire pit on the back lawn, wrapped in blankets and watching the waves dance in the moonlight. The rain had subsided just a short time ago, and everything smelled damp and fresh. The house was full of food that people just kept bringing, and Tamara had piled desserts onto a plate and brought it out with us. I'd grabbed a bottle of chardonnay and was well into my second glass. I reached for a dark chocolate fudge brownie and popped a bite in my mouth.

"It was surreal," I said through a mouthful of chocolate. I washed it down with more wine. "It was like she thought she could buy my kids."

"And fucking Skip," Tamara said, reaching for a cookie. "I knew he was a useless, cheating, rat-ass bastard, but this? This is worse than even I could have guessed."

"Shhh," I cautioned, glancing around.

The boys had taken forever to fall asleep, and I wasn't sure how fully they were out. The last thing I wanted was for them to hear us bad-mouthing their dead father.

"Sorry," Tamara said, lowering her voice to a whisper.

"I just wish I'd been pushier about getting you to leave that fucker ages ago. I mean, when the birth of your first child involves your water breaking in the presence of your naked husband and his equally-naked mistress, that's not much of an omen for good things to come."

I laughed in spite of myself.

"It's not?" I joked. "But hey – if I'd ditched him then, I wouldn't have Max."

Tamara finished her cookie and poured herself more wine, then topped off my glass.

"True," she said. "So you really only stayed with him about twelve years too long."

I stuck my tongue out at her.

"Oh, Tam, have you ever heard of a bigger mess? I mean, my head is just spinning. The lies on top of lies on top of lies, and I don't even have the luxury of trying to wrap my head around it all. I just have to find a way out."

"To that end, I have some ideas," Tamara said. "And your pal Wally does, too. He was here while you were in the study with Kitty and the Wonder Twins. He said he'll stop by tomorrow with some names you can talk to about jobs."

"That's wonderful," I said sincerely.

"And I talked to Howard on the phone a little while ago, and we agreed: you should just let Kitty take the house, and come live in Nana's cottage."

I didn't know what to say. The idea seemed wildly impractical, but it had appeal.

"Listen," Tamara went on. "Kitty doesn't want a house

in Jamestown. She's just looking for ways to take control of you and the boys. If you walk away and start over in Connecticut, it'll floor her. Odds are, she'll either offer you another deal, or put your house on the market. If she has a shred of human decency – and that's definitely an *if* – she'll give the boys the money, or use it to set up a trust fund for them or something. Right now, she just thinks she has you under her thumb, and she wants to keep you there."

"True," I agreed, watching the clouds swirl around the moon.

"So come home with me. Howard thinks he can get the boys set up at Pinecroft affordably. It might not be Max's first choice, but they do have a lacrosse team."

"The boys!" I cried, thinking of Nana's little cottage. "Where would I put them? Nana's place only has one bedroom."

"We thought of that, too," Tam said. "We've got that massive room on the third floor of the main house, and I would love to have leverage to get Howard to finally finish that bathroom up there. Eli and Max could have their own space. It would be like dorm living, right at home."

"You really want two more boys in your house?" I laughed.

"My boys think your boys are gods or something," Tam said. "And your boys are so much better-behaved than mine. This could work out for everyone."

"You don't think it will be too much, having us there?"

"I lived with you for four years at Mount Holyoke," Tam

reminded me. "And I still like you."

I smiled and reached for her hand, feeling myself begin to tear up yet again.

"You're the very best friend in the world," I said.

She squeezed my hand.

"And don't you fucking forget it," she smiled.

The ring of my iPhone startled us both. I'd forgotten I'd brought it outside with us. I picked it up and looked at the screen.

"Oh my god," I said. "Finn."

"Well, shit, answer it!" Tamara cried.

I swiped the screen and put the phone slowly to my ear.

"Eve? Eve are you there?"

"Yes, I'm here," I said.

"Look, I'm sure you're still mad at me, but please – I need to talk to you. Just give me a chance?"

I'd intended to play it cool, but I lost it immediately. I could feel tears rushing at my eyes, my sinuses flooding. Somehow, on top of everything I'd been through in the past few days, hearing his voice – his plea for forgiveness – was just too much.

"Eve? Are you okay?"

I nodded, then realized he couldn't see me through the phone.

"Yes," I said.

"You sound like you've been crying," he said, clearly concerned. "What happened?"

I laughed through my tears, thinking of all that had

transpired in the relatively short time since I'd last seen him.

"You wouldn't believe me if I told you," I said sincerely.

"Why don't you try me?" he suggested.

"Maybe another time," I said. "Tamara is consoling me with wine and baked goods."

"Tell her I said 'hi'," he said. "Call me later?"

I hesitated. I did want to call him later, but why? I'd tried calling him days ago, just as the shit hit the fan in my life, to apologize for being as harsh as I'd been with him. He hadn't answered and he hadn't called back.

Until now.

"I'll call you in a little while," I told him.

I swiped my phone off.

"What am I doing?" I moaned to Tamara. "The last thing my life needs is one more complication."

"Well," Tamara said, shrugging. "Maybe Finn won't be a complication. Evie, remember this moment. I mean it. Just take a second and breathe it in. This is it. This is as shitty as it gets, and you're still here. You've hit rock bottom, and it is all uphill from here, sister."

I did as she said. I looked around, making a mental picture of the moment: the waves jostling lightly beneath the early-fall sky, the lawn lined with gardens I'd planned and tended painstakingly over the years, the firelight dancing over the face of my best friend. I was still shell-shocked by Skip's death and the news and extent of his deception; that would take time (and probably a fair amount of therapy) to process. I would lose the house, yes, and all the work I'd put into it over the past thirteen years. I would lose the cars and the other material trappings of success. But look what remained!

I had my memories, my health, my boys. Better still, I would get to have my boys at home again, in a new home provided by the friends who had become my family over the years. I wasn't the orphan I'd thought I was when Skip proposed in my shabby little apartment. I had a family. I had Eli and Max now, and Tamara and Howard and their unruly little crew, and Nate and Ian, and Wally.

I didn't let myself think about Finn. Not yet, at least. I wasn't sure which category he would end up in: a memory filed away, or part of the makeshift family I'd assembled. It seemed too dangerous to consider.

"Go call him," Tam said, as if she'd been reading my mind. "And just because it's in my nature to be heavy-handed, I'll say this: The Red Fox is still in there somewhere, and she's a shitload of fun. Don't squash her."

I smiled as I rose from my chair. I leaned in to kiss Tamara on the cheek.

"I think she's un-squash-able," I said, and I made my way back toward the house.

In the kitchen, I swapped my wine glass for a tea cup, then headed for bed. Tucked under the covers, I called Finn. He answered seemingly before the phone could ring.

"Hey," he said. "You had me worried."

I apologized and began the long process of updating him. Even the Reader's Digest version seemed impossible. I felt like I was delivering a tale straight from an afternoon soap. When I finished, I waited.

"Woah," he said. "I really can't leave you alone for five minutes, can I?"

"Apparently not," I said.

A heavy quiet hung between us then. I thought back to the last time I'd seen him, when I'd thought the worst of him and had let him know it. I wasn't sure anything had changed, except that I was feeling more forgiving. I was feeling there was far more gray area in life than I'd previously allowed.

"You were right," he said, breaking the silence with an accurate guess at where my thoughts were drifting. "I was selfish where Molly was concerned. The going got tough and I got going. I just got lucky when Dani gave me a pass. I used that as my excuse."

"No," I said. "I was wrong. Really. I was horribly judgmental, without the least idea of what it was like to be in your shoes."

Finn chuckled, and the sound over the phone stirred something within me.

"So is this what we're going to do? Go in circles apologizing to each other?"

"So it seems," I laughed.

"Eve, I need you to let me have the last word here. I'm beyond sorry to hear what you're going through. I wish I was there..."

"Don't," I interrupted.

"I wish I was there to hold you," he insisted. "I'll be home soon."

I bit my lip and wiped at my eyes.

"Where are you?" I asked.

He paused.

"Ohio."

"Molly," I said.

"Molly," he affirmed. "I told Dani I wanted to see her, be in her life. She told her husband, believe it or not. Told him everything. He took it better than I would have."

"And they've agreed to let you see her?"

"Sort of. I told you the new dad is a shrink? He thinks it would be harmful to tell her the truth. He suggested I be her long-lost uncle. Like I was going to be when I died, I suppose, only without the whole, pesky death part."

I thought about that.

"You'd be lying to her in person, then."

"Right. As opposed to in absentia, which I've done her whole life."

I wasn't sure which was worse. Still, I thought it was something that Finn was there. He was making an effort he wouldn't have made before. Had I done that? Had I guilted him into it?

"How uncomfortable are you right now?" I asked impulsively.

"I'm crawling out of my skin," he said, laughing uneasily.

"Yeah, I guessed this was out of your comfort zone." I paused. "It's a good thing."

"Hey, can you go on Face Time?" he asked.

I thought of how I must look.

"Oh no," I said.

"Please?"

We hung up, and I quickly tried to make myself presentable: smoothing my hair, rubbing at the circles under my eyes, sitting up a bit. Then there we were, both of us shot at an unflattering angle, yet somehow I understood why he'd done it.

"Hi, you," he said.

"Hey," I smiled.

I had missed his face, I realized. Was that possible? I'd hardly known him long enough for that to seem rational.

"It is so nice to see you," he said, echoing my thoughts. "You look beautiful."

"You're ruining your credibility, you know," I said. "I can only imagine what I look like right now."

"Eh, well, all right. Maybe not beautiful, but not half bad considering," he smirked. "How's that?"

"Better," I chuckled.

I tried to frame it all: we'd buried Skip that morning, I'd learned of all his lies this afternoon, and now I was looking up Finn's nose on Face Time as I lay in bed. What the hell kind of world was this?

"I've really got to get some sleep," I told him, unable to think of anything else to say.

"I'll be home on Saturday," he said. "Could I take you

out to dinner?"

Oh, how I wanted to say yes.

"I don't think so," I said. "A lot is up in the air for us right now. I don't even know where the boys and I will be by Saturday."

"Can I call you tomorrow, then?" he asked, not missing a beat.

I nodded.

"That would be nice," I said sincerely.

"Sweet dreams, Eve," he said.

I leaned into my pillows.

"Good night, Finn," I said.

I ended the call and set the phone down. Then I lay there, the bedside light on, and blinked back the tears I was sick of crying.

Chapter **Twelve**

I went to the Wolcott home in Newport to, as Tamara suggested, tell Kitty to "go fuck herself." I waited in the foyer and then was shown into the conservatory, where Kitty sat amidst roses carefully tended by her gardener. She was dressed in pastels and her thin frame nearly floated on a tufted chaise. She looked almost frail, if you didn't know her.

"Come in," she said. "Close the door behind you. Have a seat."

I sat at a table across from her.

"I'll be brief," I said. "I'm not interested in your offer. If you won't decline the trusteeship and allow me to take control of the home I've raised my boys in, then I don't really care what you do with the house. I've made arrangements to move to Connecticut and enroll Max and Eli in an excellent school there. You see, they're my children, and if you think you can take them from me, you are sorely mistaken."

Kitty looked flustered, but only for a moment.

"Don't be ridiculous," she said. "No one is looking to

take your children or your home away from you. I'm just offering the help you clearly need. Your recent lapses in judgment, and your appalling behavior..."

"Are none of your fucking business, Kitty."

"Tsk, tsk, there you go with the language again." She rolled her eyes. "I just don't understand you girls these days. Do you think I don't know my son had a wandering eye? That apple didn't fall far from the tree. His father was the very same way. In fact, Skip himself was conceived when I needed to remind my husband of his obligations. But did I ever make a fuss? Talk divorce? Resort to *unladylike* behavior?

"Of course not. It just wasn't done in my day, and there's no need for it now. A patient wife has no end of tools at her disposal, you know. Denying her thoughtless husband his creature comforts, for example. Cheap scotch substituted for his favorite. Slippers a half size too small. Dinner served at the wrong time. Burnt toast with his tea.

"And then life gives you little gifts," she added, turning to look at her roses. "A terminal illness is such a nasty thing, and so difficult on the caregiver. Especially when you look at the patient and see the man who humiliated you so, carrying on with every damned nurse in the hospital so that everyone – everyone – on the board knew.

"But then you see how that man has been weakened by illness. You see how fully dependant upon you he has become. What can he do if you give him his pain medication every six hours instead of every four? Or if you miss a dose altogether? Or if, in the very end, you decide you've just had enough of your house smelling like a goddamned hospital, and so you help things along with an extra dose or two.

"These are the things a wife can do, Eve. These are the ways of setting the balance right. Nothing public or messy. Certainly no cavorting on the beach with strangers. No! Just a quiet shifting of the scales in favor of the party who's been wronged."

I sat, rooted in silence and chilled to the bone, for a long time.

"Kitty," I said at last, my voice almost a whisper. "You did those things to Dr. Wolcott? Tormented him during his final illness? Overdosed and killed him, even?"

Kitty waved a hand at me.

"There you go with the melodrama again. Did you hear a thing I said? I did nothing that man didn't have coming, and I did it all quietly. I spared the family further embarrassment, and I made certain my husband felt sorry for all the hurt he'd caused. He apologized, oh, he did! Look at the circus you've created. Don't you see the benefit of my way? Isn't it clear?"

Something was clear, of that I was sure. Two somethings, even.

One: Kitty was far worse than I'd ever imagined. She was pure evil.

Two: When Tamara instructed me to record my conversation with Kitty "just in case," she'd given me the gift of a lifetime.

I extracted my phone from my pocket and tapped to save the recording. I tapped again to email it to Tamara and

Wally. I was shaking as I considered how the tables had suddenly turned.

"Kitty, you remember those pictures you showed me? How careful you were to be sure I understood that the prints were backed up by a digital file?"

She said nothing, but realization seemed to be dawning. Her mole-studded face crumpled.

"I recorded everything you just said, and I've already emailed it off to a few people. I wanted to be sure our conversation was documented so you couldn't pull one of your nasty tricks, but I've got to be honest, I had no idea just how nasty you are. Just as I'm sure no one at the ladies' auxiliary or on the hospital board or in any of the other organizations with which you're involved would imagine. I mean, truly: imagine! Never mind the possibility of criminal charges for your behavior. Just think of the social crucifixion. You'd be a pariah. And talk about damage to the family name!"

"That's enough," she said, her voice strangled. "I suppose you're going to blackmail me now. What do you want?"

"Kitty, I want exactly what I wanted from the start. Control of my home and my children. And you know what? That tuition money for the boys would be nice, too. Only I'll decide at which school it gets spent. That only seems fair."

Kitty sat stiffly, her eyes fixed on a point beyond the roses lining the windows.

232

"I'll have the attorneys draw up the paperwork," she said at last, apparently determined to play as if it were nothing. "You can show yourself out."

I turned to go.

"You know," Kitty said as I reached the door. I paused, my hand on the knob. "I never thought much of you."

I turned and looked at her, waiting. Was she about to admit she'd been wrong? Had beating her at her own twisted game finally given me some sort of worth in her eyes?

She leveled her steely gaze at me.

"I was right, of course," she said coolly. Her eyes drifted away as if I didn't warrant her full attention. "You've no class at all. The only good I can find in any of this is that poor Skip is finally free of you."

I turned my back.

"Goodbye, Kitty," I said, and I closed the door behind me.

Suddenly, my life was all about change.

Kitty resigned as successor trustee, leaving me in charge of the Jamestown house. I put it on the market and proceeded with my plans to move into Nana's cottage in Stonington. I traded in Skip's Range Rover and my trio of BMWs for a green Subaru Outback wagon with all-wheel drive and a rack for my paddle board.

Max prevailed upon me to let him return to Morefield, and I relented. It wasn't my first choice, but he was happy there, and it was his father's and grandfather's alma mater. Eli, of course, was thrilled with his interview at Pinecrest, and they were just as happy with him. He could have his new room in Tamara and Howard's house and I could drive him to school every day. We were both on cloud nine, though for entirely different reasons.

"Did you see the photography studio, Mom?" he asked excitedly on the drive back from his Pinecrest interview.

I'm sure I had, but all I could see in that moment was the smile spread wide across my melancholy boy's face.

Wally came out of retirement swinging. Within a week he had interviews lined up for me at six different law firms, all of whom seemed unusually accommodating of a forty-ish lawyer who'd practiced for only six months nearly fourteen years ago. I had him to tea to let him down easy.

"Wally, you're a doll, so please don't think I am unappreciative of your efforts," I said. "But what would you think if I said I'd been offered a different kind of job?"

"Different how?"

"Volunteer coordinator for the animal rescue league?"

I probably should have offered him Scotch instead of tea.

"Really? You want to shovel dog shit instead of wearing a suit and racking up billable hours?"

"C'mon, Wally," I said wryly, leveling a gaze at him. "You and I both know we're just talking about two different

234

varieties of shit-shoveling."

A smile tugged at the corners of the deep-set lines framing his mouth.

"Kiddo, you might just be better off with the dog shit," he allowed.

"Really, it doesn't mean I'm not grateful for your efforts," I said gently. "I know how lucky I am to have a friend like you."

He waved a hand at me.

"I'm too goddamned old to take much of anything personally. Just be happy, okay?"

I smiled.

"I'm calling that 'Plan A'," I assured him.

Tamara expressed gratitude that our move had motivated Howard to finish work on the third floor bedroom and bathroom, as if we were the ones doing them the favor.

"Fucker starts five billion projects all at once. Damned if he finishes one of them," she said.

"And by 'fucker,' you mean your husband and the father of your four children?" I teased.

She shrugged.

"It's an affectionate term. He finished that piss sculpture, you know. He's almost normal again. I feel like it's safe to suck his dick again."

"Geez, Tam," I cried. "TMI!"

"You feel downright ordinary, now, though, don't you?" she asked. "All that weird shit in your life lately – you're secretly thinking it's not so odd, right? So, you're welcome."

We dissolved in laughter.

And Finn?

Fall turned to winter, and I kept Finn at a distance. We talked on the phone and on FaceTime now and then, and I'd be lying if I said I didn't want to see him in person, didn't long to touch and smell and taste him. I knew how he'd make me melt, and truly, I longed for that feeling. It was simply a variable for which I couldn't allow. Not just yet.

Eli and Max were each in the right place now, school-wise at least, but they struggled with their grief over the loss of their father. I was trying to gain my footing in my new job, balancing work and parenthood for the first time ever in my life. There were days I wanted to write a blog entitled, "How the Hell Do You Do It?" directed at single mothers, but I guessed there probably wasn't much of a sympathetic readership out there. Subconsciously or not, I'd chosen carefully when I'd stayed with Skip over the years. Parenthood wasn't for sissies under the best of circumstances, and single parenthood? Damn, pin a medal on those folks, every one of them, if they managed to raise a reasonably upstanding member of society.

Between my work (which I loved, as it turned out – shit-shoveling and all) and driving Eli to and from Pinecrest and his various activities, I made Nana's cottage my own. I painted the kitchen and made room for all my favorite family photos. In

236

packing up the Jamestown house I'd found the quilt Nana made when I'd graduated Mount Holyoke. It lay on my bed now, comforting in all respects.

I'd found something else when packing to move. In the library, crumpled into the corner of a drawer of Skip's desk, I'd found the beginnings of a letter in his handwriting.

Eve, I am so sorry. I don't know what is wrong with me. I don't deserve you. I know that, but I love you. Truly I do. I'm so sorry.

His writing had trailed off, the ink was smeared, and the paper smelled faintly of Scotch. There was no date, nothing to discern when he'd written it, but I guessed it hadn't been long ago. I sat there and cried, though for myself or for Skip, I couldn't say. I ran my hands over the page, picturing him writing those words, probably while solidly drunk, yet still they felt like something of a gift. He'd done too much damage for me to forgive him just yet, but knowing he'd felt some remorse for some aspect of his misbehavior softened a corner of my heart. I'd tucked the letter into a box destined for storage.

In the quiet of night, when I snuggled in under Nana's quilt, I felt mostly hopeful. But sometimes there was a little twinge, a tug of sadness I couldn't quite explain. Was it for Skip? Or did I miss Nana, whose presence I felt so fully in the cottage?

Or was it something else entirely?

I turned forty the day after Christmas.

Was there any worse day in the world for a birthday?

It was anticlimactic under the best of circumstances, but since first my father, then my mother, had passed in early December, my birthday became a hopelessly bleak event. I'd stopped celebrating long ago. It was a day of department-store returns. A day when people with family ate leftovers and visiting relatives struggled not to wear out their welcome. A day of snow turned to slush, and the beginning of a tired slog toward a new year.

Tam and Howard insisted on having a cake for me – a vegan chocolate delight that I'd have been hard-pressed to turn down. Nate and Ian were visiting for the holidays and somehow convinced the kids to collaborate on a delightfully campy production of "Tomorrow" from the musical *Annie*. Warhol shone in the title role, and Max good-naturedly donned drag and hammed it up in the role of Miss Hannigan. Eli served as stage manager, though I could tell it was all he could do not to collapse in laughter when Max ordered the "orphans" to polish the floor to a Chrysler-building shine.

Not a bad birthday, all in all.

I kissed my boys goodnight as they dodged me on their way up to their lair on the third floor of the main house. Then I wrapped my wool sweater about me and dashed through the chill to Nana's cottage.

Snow was falling lightly, sparse flakes punctuating the dark of night. The air smelled of wood smoke and solitude. I paused at the edge of the pond, the thin sheet of ice crossing the surface split by frost. I tried to recall the feeling of panic that had fluttered within me so many times recently – when I'd been served with divorce papers, when I'd learned Skip had died, when I'd watched Kitty crumple under the news that her son had bankrupted himself and left his family with nothing.

So many times, the world had ended.

And yet it hadn't.

I left the pond and let myself into the cottage. The fire in the wood stove had died down, and I stoked it with more logs. I shook my sweater off onto a chair, watching the snowflakes melt into the knit. I yawned and headed to the bathroom to change.

A noise just outside stopped me.

Voices?

I opened the door and clapped a hand to my mouth, stunned. I found myself laughing and fighting back tears all at once.

Finn stood there, holding his iPhone out, Lou Reed's "Perfect Day" blaring through the tinny speaker. Bessie sat parked on the lawn of the cottage, tire tracks studding the light fall of snow in her wake.

"What on earth are you doing?" I asked.

"Well," he said, lowering the phone and glancing about awkwardly. "I was thinking of the whole John Cusack/*Say*

Anything boombox scene. But I don't have a boombox. And I like Lou Reed better than Peter Gabriel. And it's really not the same when you're on the first floor, so I can't do the whole, dramatic holding-it-over-my-head-and-looking-up-at-you-longingly thing. And it's not raining. And you're prettier than Ione Skye, and..."

"Oh, shut up," I said, pulling him to me.

Lou Reed was muffled as the phone was caught somewhere between us. I pressed my nose into Finn's neck, breathing deeply. I felt the warmth of his body and understood how fully I had missed him. It didn't matter if it made little sense, or if he had flaws that should have given a rational person pause. My connection to him defied logic, and I knew in that moment that it transcended the physical.

It wasn't just that he'd been there when I'd been ready – at long last – to break free of my good-girl mold. It was something about the combination of the two of us together. His wild abandon, my dutiful nature. The desire each of us had for greater balance. The way we'd each stepped outside our comfort zones when we met one another. We'd leapt from the precipice; there was no going back. But now here we were, with each other to cling to. Hopefully not in a life-raft sort of way. Maybe more as a kind of bolster or cheering section.

"I know you don't want to hear this, Eve," he said, his lips little more than an inch from mine. "You need your space, and I am doing my damnedest to respect that. But here's the thing: I am falling in love with you. I mean, I've fallen. I mean..."

"Finn..." I started.

He dropped his head. When he looked up, something in his eyes silenced me.

"I love you," he said. "I can't recall the last time those words passed my lips. Maybe I'm foolish for saying them now, but the thing is, whether this is something that will pass and I'll feel stupid or something that will end with us side-by-side in rocking chairs at some old folks' home somewhere in the distant future, I feel it now. I can't imagine anything I wouldn't do to keep feeling this way, and maybe that makes me a masochist, because it's hurt like hell to stay away since you asked me to. But at the same time, I'm so impressed by the person I see you working to become. I just want to be part of that."

I bit my lip and swallowed the lump that had risen in my throat.

"Oh, Finn," I said, grasping for words. "I feel the same way. Maybe I'm stupid to trust you – to trust anyone – after all I've gone through with Skip, but I can't seem to help myself. I think you're a bigger person than you allow yourself to believe. I believe in you, I really do, and I hope that's not a mistake." I drew a deep breath. "But it's a chance I'm willing to take."

I felt his body relax against mine, as if he'd released an enormous burden in a single sigh.

"Eve," he murmured, burying his face in my neck.

I felt it, then – his heart beating through the thin fabric of his tee shirt. His chiseled muscles wrapped in tattoos seemed suddenly like a façade I'd peeled away. This was the real Finn, the man who held me in his arms now. He was warm and vulnerable and still, he was my superhero. He'd conquered his fear and opened a door to his past, welcoming his daughter into his life in spite of all the strings attached, in spite of the potential danger of the tangled web he himself had woven. He'd come after me when I'd retreated. He'd taken the chance that connecting himself to others might limit his freedom. He'd allowed that the rewards might be worth it.

"I love you, Finn," I said, my voice barely a whisper.

He took the breath out of me, enclosing me in an embrace so fervent and passionate I gasped. His fingertips traveled down my spine, and I felt the need rise in me.

"There's one more thing," he whispered, drawing back.

Disappointment was replaced by curiosity as he retreated to his truck, leaving me shivering in the doorway. He returned with a blanket-wrapped bundle clutched to his chest.

"Happy Birthday, Eve," he said.

I gasped as the bundle began to wriggle. Carefully, I peeled back a corner of the blanket. A little black nose poked out at me, followed by a sweet fawn-colored face. A Leonberger pup.

"Oh, you didn't!" I breathed.

"Don't worry. I cleared it with your landlord."

"Tamara knew about this!" I cried.

Finn nodded.

"They had a whole litter of them at an animal rescue in Ohio. He was the only male, and I read something that said the males bark less than the females, so…"

I scooped the puppy out of Finn's arms. The little dog

lapped happily at my face.

"Oh," I whispered, speechless. I pulled Finn into the cottage and closed the door, primarily so the puppy wouldn't be cold. "You... I can't believe..."

The sly, dead-sexy smile that had done me in from the start crossed Finn's face.

"Well, I heard nothing gets the job done like a puppy on a string," he said. "You're done-for now, right?"

I punched him on the arm, then leaned in, burying my face in his neck. The puppy went to work licking both of our faces.

"I've been calling him Sammy," Finn said, gently cupping the pup's face and laughing as he tried to stop him from licking. "I thought it sounded like Sally, but good for a little boy-dog. But I don't think he knows his name yet. You could name him whatever you want."

I tucked the puppy into one of Nana's quilts in front of the wood stove. He settled down, curling into a ball with his face tilted toward the fire.

"No," I said. "I like Sammy. That suits him." Then I paused, thinking of something. "Wait -- you had him at your house? What did Oscar Wilde think of that?"

Finn laughed.

"Ah, see, there's just one more reason you have to spend more time with me. Sammy and Oscar Wilde are fast friends. They were chasing each other all over the house."

"You're kidding!"

"Not at all. Oscar Wilde was positively kittenish. Or

puppyish, actually. I threw a ball for Sammy, and Oscar beat him to it. I now have a cat who can fetch."

"Well, if Sammy can teach Oscar to fetch, maybe Oscar can teach Sammy to paddle board," I suggested.

I looked over at the tiny ball of fluff curled contentedly before the fire. Sammy sighed and stretched, reaching an impressively large paw out of the blanket. He would weigh over a hundred pounds in no time. He'd need his own board.

"Wait 'til the boys see him," I said. "They'll be over the moon."

"Are you over the moon?" Finn asked.

"I am," I said sincerely. "You know, you didn't even need the puppy. You had me at, 'I was thinking of John Cusack.'"

Finn chuckled.

"You're too easy, you know that?" he said.

I took him by the hand and led him toward the bedroom.

"Oh, and let me show you how," I said.

Chapter **Thirteen**

This is how I remember New Year's Day:

At breakfast, Nate and Ian told us the news. After years of trying to adopt a baby, they'd met with success of a different kind. They were adopting a pair of twelve year old girls, twins who'd spent too long in foster care and seemed destined to age out of the system.

"It will be a different kind of family," Ian said haltingly.

"But then," Nate continued with a smile. "We're different."

I looked at my boys, Max gleefully needling Eli as he fiddled with settings on the camera he'd gotten for Christmas. I said a silent prayer of thanks for couples like Nate and Ian, wise enough to recognize that there were a million ways to build a family, and that kids this age needed security as much as any infant.

We ate pancakes and vegan bacon while Tamara and Howard's wild brood ran to and from the table, happy little hellions, then we piled into cars and caravanned to the beach. I spotted Bessie in the crowded parking lot, Finn behind the wheel. The reedy, dark-haired beauty beside him could only be Molly.

"Hey," Finn called, climbing from the truck and coming to meet us. "Happy New Year. This is Molly. My, um, niece."

I smiled and shook her hand.

"Ever do anything like this before?" I asked her.

She shook her head, smiling.

"It's kind of crazy," she said. "But fun. I just probably won't tell my mom about this."

I laughed. The boys ran riot, waving and calling for us to hurry up. We followed them down to the water's edge.

As the clock ticked toward noon, we stripped down to our swimsuits, leaving our boots and winter coats in the snowdrifts topping the sand. Tamara handed me a flask.

"Fuck me, here we go again," she cried as I took a swig.

Twenty years earlier, Tamara and I had done our first New Year's Day plunge together, holding hands and running on skinny legs into the freezing surf as Nana and her parents watched from the beach.

Now here we were again, less skinny and more than a dozen strong, carried along with the crowd but clinging to each other still: Tamara with three little boys clustered at her feet, Howard with the littlest one clutched to his chest, Nate pulling Ian along, ever-reluctant, Max vying for position alongside Molly, Eli shaking loose of my grasp, and Finn catching my eye a split-second before he caught my hand.

246

"Three, two, one!" the crowd chanted, then the mad dash into the ocean began.

This is it, I thought, looking around me at the laughing, crazy group of people I loved. *This is life.*

We dove into the surf, the icy water stinging and knocking the breath from us, but I had no doubt we would all surface. It would hurt, and we'd come out with our skin red and smarting, but then we'd shake it off and the new year would begin.

Acknowledgements

First: many, many thanks to my editor and friend Cynthia Drummond, who kindly went through this manuscript with her red pencil and her keen eye, both of which were much-needed.

Thanks to Gary McCluskey, whose talent continues to impress me – I am so thrilled with the beautiful cover. Everything I dreamed of, and not a zombie or werewolf in sight!

Thanks to the friends/cheerleaders who toughed out the writing and revision process with me, offering encouragement, feedback and wine as needed: Tiphany Giles, Stephanie White, Jacy Northup, Sue DeSiato, Sue Christiano, Julie Ladd, Linda LaCamera, Erin Naig, Eppie Leishman, Katie Mooney, Joanna Kercz, Katherine "Bean" Pontes, Kristen McDonough, Kristen Marie Antonio, Kristen Ann Antonio and everyone else who was so totally awesome while I worked my tail off.

Thanks to Jennifer Hodge at Spectrum Makeup Artistry, Jeannine Denecour at Advanced Hair Design, and Michelle Dimery at Dimery Photography for making me look my best for author pics and promotions.

Thanks to my Mom, Karen Kuhn Antonio, for believing in me the way only a mom can. And thanks to my mother- and father-in-law, Anne & David Forber, who bemusedly encouraged me to tell them ALL about this book in spite of Andrew's embarrassment. (Anne, rest assured and thank god, you are no Kitty Wolcott!)

Thanks to Andrew and Ryan, who put up with everything from the constant clacking of my keyboard to the absence of groceries in the fridge, and who more or less bit their tongues when they heard the title and subject matter of this book. There may be fifty ways to leave your husband, but there are countless ways I love you guys.

Last but most definitely not least, thanks to my amazing online family – the friends who support me via Facebook, Twitter, Goodreads, Tumblr and all the other places we bookworms find community in cyberspace. Thank you for your enthusiasm for my work, and for the time you take to share with friends, write reviews and post to get my name out there in the world. I literally could not do this without your support. I am grateful every day that you've got my back.

1,4,3...
- k.c.
August 2013
Rhode Island

About the Author

k.c. wilder is the author of the novel Fifty Ways to Leave Your Husband. She lives in Rhode Island with her husband, her son, two dogs and a cat, all of whom are deeply embarrassed that she's written a book with so dang many sex scenes. She'd love it if you'd check out her web site, "like" her on Facebook, follow her on Twitter or subscribe to her blog on Tumblr.

www.kcwilder50ways.com

Made in the USA
Charleston, SC
15 May 2014